ZOMBIE ATTACK: TORONTO

B. T. CLABBY

authorHOUSE

AuthorHouse™ UK
1663 Liberty Drive
Bloomington, IN 47403 USA
www.authorhouse.co.uk
Phone: UK TFN: 0800 0148641 (Toll Free inside the UK)
*   UK Local: (02) 0369 56322 (+44 20 3695 6322 from outside the UK)*

Published by AuthorHouse   11/18/2021

ISBN: 978-1-6655-9205-5 (sc)
ISBN: 978-1-6655-9206-2 (hc)
ISBN: 978-1-6655-9207-9 (e)

CHAPTER 1

George and I had been out checking trails for about four hours and had covered sixteen of my sites when he began acting strangely. George, by the way, was my dog, a six-year-old Border collie who had a Canadian Kennel Club ranking for his breed (my wife's doing) and as a scent tracker (my doing).

I ran a hunt camp in central Ontario, just outside a small town called, of all names, Huntsville. It was only a couple of hours' drive north of Toronto, the fourth-largest city in North America. It was beautiful country nestled in the Canadian Shield, with plenty of clean lakes, rivers, and forest for fishing and game hunting. I had seventeen hundred acres of this prime forest, with a private lake that bordered thousands of acres of other prime lakes and forest.

It was late in February. In today's environment, I used technology to assist in tracking the movement of my customers' prey. I also did what was called "seeding" certain tracks to encourage the deer and other animals to use those same trails. I knew some people would say that wasn't fair, but it provided food and nutrients to animals through the often-harsh winter months. And yes, it did allow me to set up blinds (locations that were camouflaged or hidden from the prey) that provided my paying clientele a better than good chance of bagging a deer, elk, or maybe even a moose. You must look at things realistically; groups of hunters aren't going to return to a location if they won't have a successful hunt.

1

Back to the technology—I also used twenty 7-megapixel game cameras with infrared lenses to help track which prey were going where. These cameras were able to video any object that triggered the motion sensors within fifteen meters (fifty feet). I could then use some extra seeding on those trails to help encourage more travel or, conversely, abandon unused trails in that section. I then downloaded any videos to my iPad for later research and planning.

My camp had seven cabins that I rented out, with room for up to ten guests, with four cabins usually sleeping six people, as that was the most typical size for a hunting party. The cabins had been mostly booked for the spring hunt season, but I still had some vacancies. I figured I would check my emails for the company when I got back from checking the trails. I checked twice a week to limit contamination of the trails by my scent. I would often use an eight-wheeled Argo on my rounds, as I found it was a lot quieter than a snowmobile and would cross water without sinking.

Anyway, George started acting funny as we pulled up to the seventeenth trail camera. As I went to check the camera, I told him to be quiet so as not to scare any deer nearby, but he kept barking and jumping on his hind legs between me and something farther up the trail. After failing to calm him down, I came up beside him to pat down his raised hackles. He took a quick look up at me as I petted him and then turned his attention back up the trail. It was then I caught a smell—an ugly smell, the smell of decaying meat.

I began to walk up the trail slowly, turning my head from side to side, watching for any sign of movement. George would take about four steps and then stop, sniff the air, and look back to me until I gave the hand sign for him to go forward, and he obliged. We followed this routine for about ten meters until we came across the carcass of a buck. It looked like it had been a fine specimen, three to four years old, fifty-five to seventy kilos in weight. Its state of decomposition indicated that it had been dead for two or three days. But what was most disturbing to me, aside from the waste of a fine specimen, was the apparent manner of its death. The head had been ripped from its body.

At first, I thought it might have been a bear attack, but I quickly realized the bears were still hibernating. I grabbed my iPad out of my backpack and began taking pictures of the torn carcass and then went back to the game cam(era) to download the data, as the attack had occurred within its fifteen-meter scan. With a predator like this on the loose, I needed to get back to my cabin quickly to report my findings to the local authorities. So George and I quickly got back to the Argo and raced back home. The other trails could wait till the next day.

It took forty-five minutes to get back to my personal cabin. I started the gas stove for a kettle of hot water to make some hot chocolate. Then I fired up my old computer and got the cables ready to hook up my iPad. By the time everything was ready, the kettle was boiling, and I made myself the hot chocolate and gave George his treat of a raw frozen turkey drumstick.

As I began reviewing my game cam videos, I made note of the trails made by the deer and elk. I noticed my computer was offline. I would have to call my internet provider as soon as I had finished monitoring all the videos. As I was putting the phone to my ear, however, the scene from the seventeenth camera came on the monitor. I stared at the screen as a four-point buck came strolling into view. It was a magnificent creature, with antlers reaching some seven feet, weighing a guesstimate of 150 pounds, and strong shoulders and a muscular hind. The infrared showed a good strong heart and lungs. Then with the phone still to my ear, I saw a sudden motion, the type you often see in the old horror movies, as something or someone attacked from the side.

The attack didn't last but a minute, and the poor animal was dead in a matter of seconds, as could be seen by the infrared monitor projecting directly below the video footage. I slowly set the phone down on the desk and sat for I don't know how long, just staring at the computer monitor until George stuck his wet nose into my hand. This made me jump and brought me out of my daze, though my mind still would not let me believe what I had just witnessed. Just to try to be sure, I watched the video over again and felt sick to see the deer being ripped apart. It had happened so quickly the deer didn't appear to have suffered, but something else about the video now bothered me. I couldn't put my finger on it, but something was wrong—very wrong.

I then watched the video for a third time with some stop and go for closer observation. As I did, I again picked up the phone, with the intention of calling the conservation officer. It was then I noticed I had no dial tone. I hung up and tried the phone again with the same results— no dial tone.

This was strange. Things were increasingly growing strange as I played the video over again. I paused the footage just as the deer was being attacked. Although the picture was a bit grainy owing to the distance, I saw what appeared to be two human attackers. I wondered how these two were able to get so close to a wild deer. Then, still looking at the still photo, I noticed what it was about the video that disturbed me so much—these attackers had no heat signatures!

As I fixated on the computer screen, I absently picked up the phone for a third time but still got no dial tone. No internet either when I checked the toolbar on the computer. I live about thirty kilometers out of town, and the sun was already setting. Both the conservation office and the provincial police station were on the other side of town, and neither would be manned overnight during the winter months. Without someone to see the video, how was I going to explain to some radio dispatcher what I had seen and why I needed help? I would sound like a nutcase. Long lonely winter nights had that effect on some people.

Dark clouds had been gathering all day, and even without the internet, I knew we were in for another winter storm. It started about four that afternoon with freezing rain followed by hail. There was no way I was going back out in those conditions. I kept trying to rationalize or otherwise talk myself out of what I had seen on that video. It was impossible—some sort of trick or malfunction. Perhaps the heat sensor wasn't working. Or it was a bear that had attacked the deer? These explanations didn't pass muster, and I knew it. The heat sensor did show heat from the deer, so it must have been functioning. And bears were hibernating this time of year and not easily awakened. As Arthur C. Doyle's great detective Sherlock Holmes often said, "Once you eliminate the impossible, whatever remains, however improbable, must be the truth."

By now, the wind was howling, and the steady thump of the icy rain and hail now battered the cabin. My hot chocolate had gone cold while I was trying to understand what I had seen on the video. I lowered the aluminum screens on the outside to protect the windows, reheated my dinner, and started a fire in the fireplace. I was low on firewood inside, so I went out to gather more from the lean-to just outside the cabin. Just then, the power went out, throwing everything into darkness. After about two minutes, my back-up generator kicked into life to give me about 60 percent of my normal power usage. I knew I would have between two and four days of power, depending on how much I drew.

No phone, no internet, and now no power I was batting a thousand. I did, however, have one last chance to communicate with the outside world should I choose to use it. My old CB radio didn't rely on modern technology. CB radios work either on-line of sight or relay system, which doesn't require the same level of technology as, say, cellular or smartphones (ever seen how smart a smartphone is during a power failure?) I figured I had enough bad luck for one day and, with the storm beginning to pour down, decided to wait till morning before trying it if the phone and internet were still out of service. I decided as the attack appeared to be a couple of days old, I wasn't in imminent danger. Nor was there anything I could do at that moment. So, I decided to just go to bed and get some sleep.

As I crossed the room, I passed the gun case and stopped. For some reason I can't explain other than an awfully bad feeling, I took several guns out of the cabinet and loaded them. I didn't chamber any rounds, but each magazine was loaded and ready to go with only a second's action. I'm at a loss to explain why, but I had a feeling of unease. For the first time since serving in the army, I went to bed with loaded weapons.

My sleep that night was restless, as George kept getting up at the smallest of sounds. Finally, around 3:00 a.m., there was a banging at my window, and George started barking. I got up and moved around the room, cradling a shotgun in my arms. As I got close to the window, I noticed the wind was still howling. So, I told George, and myself, it was just the hail being blown against the shutters. Nevertheless, I turned on several lights and threw more wood on the fire. Then deciding sleep was out of the question, I sat in a rocking chair rather than going back to bed. Here, I stared into the fire, hypnotized by the flame, and rocking back and forth, unable to rid my mind of the horror of the video. My mind went back in time to when I was a soldier and responsible for the FOO (forward observation officer) in my commando unit.

I must have dozed off, for the next thing I knew, it was 7:00 a.m., and I had given up on any chance for a proper sleep. So I put on some coffee. Then I went to check on the phone and internet to see if either were working. They weren't—service still hadn't been restored. I figured it wouldn't be till much later in the day before work crews would be able to restore service so decided to try my luck with the CB radio.

I turned it on and waited for it to warm up, took the mike in hand, depressed the talk switch, and broadcast, "Breaker, breaker one-nine, anyone on the air this morning? Come back." CB has a total language of its own. The term *breaker*, for instance, is used to interrupt regular chatter. *One-nine* refers to the channel being used—in this case, 19; it is also the most common channel on which to initiate a conversation. And *come back* simply tells people you are finished with your transmission, and the air is free for a reply.

After the break, I gave a few minutes for a reply but got nothing. I sent the message out again but still didn't receive any reply. Either there was no one within range of my transmission or, most likely, my antenna was covered in ice from the storm. The wind was still strong, but it looked like the precipitation had finally let up.

I began putting on my boots, hat, and jacket and headed for the door. I noticed my handgun was on the table. It was a Desert Eagle .50 caliber. I looked down at it sitting there and, for some reason, felt myself pick it up and looked at it in my hand. I told myself I didn't need the gun. I was just going out to the antenna, which was only ten meters from the cabin. The gun felt heavy in my hands, and I wasn't even sure when I picked it up or why, it was just an eerie feeling came over me. Then, once I was outside, I chambered its first round.

George accompanied me to the tower that had the antenna for the CB radio, and I cleared away the ice from it. We both seemed to have our eyes and ears peeled for any unusual sights or sounds. The ground was icy, and we both slipped and slid along the path. Halfway back to my cabin, I stopped dead in my tracks thinking I had heard something. George also stopped and with his head popped up to listen better. He looked up at me with nervous eyes. The forest was so quiet I could hear

George's breathing, which was when I noticed I needed to take a breath as well. The total stillness and quiet were unnatural, even in the dead of winter.

Somewhere behind me was a loud crack, followed by a bang. I spun around and went into a combat crouch, bringing my Desert Eagle up to a two-handed firing position. My left foot slipped out from under me on the ice, and I went down hard on my back. George, at the same moment, had let out a loud bark and then came over to me on the ground and began to lick my face as I was letting out a few choice words. I pushed George out of the way while trying to get back onto my feet from my all fours.

Off to my right some twenty meters away, a young Douglas fir had succumbed to the heavy ice that had saturated its branches from the storm the night before. Laughing I stroked George's head and said to him, "Look at the two of us, George—big-time hunt guides being spooked by a falling tree. Well, I guess that answers the question, If a tree falls in the forest, does it make any sound?" I holstered the Desert Eagle and slowly continued up the path to the cabin.

Once back in the cabin, I checked the phone and internet again, but they were still down. Then I tried the CB radio but only got more static. I knew the antenna was now free of ice, so this puzzled me. Not very often that happens. But it does occasionally. So I changed to channel 9. This is the emergency channel, which is supposed to be monitored by the police around the clock. After trying channel 9 for ten minutes with still no results, I was confused. I knew I was within range of the police station in town, so there should have been some acknowledgement.

CHAPTER 2

Things seemed to be going from bad to worse. I first thought much of the problem was a result of the night's ice storm. That type of situation had occurred several times in the past, more frequently now with global warming. The sky was heavily overcast and looked like more freezing rain was possible at any time. I decided my only choice was to go into town myself to make the report. I got the keys to my Humvee 2 in the garage and then checked my two handguns. Both had full magazines. I placed the Browning 9mm in the back of my jeans, and the Desert Eagle I placed in the glove compartment.

George and I got into the SUV and then headed over the dirt road that served as my private driveway for one and a half kilometers to the main highway. The going was slippery, and I partially slid off the road a few times before finally getting to the highway. It, too, was still covered in ice, and I wondered why it hadn't been cleared or salted yet. I guessed it was my tax dollars at work again. The Humvee is a heavy vehicle, and with the specialty snow tires I had invested in, it was able to keep reasonable traction on the road; but there were a few times I almost ditched the vehicle. As a result, I lowered my speed, making the twenty-minute trip to town take nearly an hour.

As I made my way into town, I noticed the traffic lights were out, and there appeared to be no other vehicles on the road, which was good, as my Humvee slid through the intersection despite my best efforts to come to a stop. I arrived at the conservation office and slid a few times as I walked up to the front entrance and found the door locked. I wasn't sure what I expected really, considering the weather conditions, but frustration and a feeling of dread were evident. Something just wasn't feeling quite right.

This feeling of unease intensified as I drove to the police station shortly afterward and found their doors locked as well. There was a phone beside the door that was supposed to connect directly to the police dispatcher to use in case of an emergency. I decided this was such a time. I lifted the receiver, and the phone began to ring on the other end. It rang and rang and rang but still went unanswered. I must have waited a good ten minutes for a response but got nothing.

As I stood outside the police station pondering my situation, something finally got my attention. I hadn't seen a living soul all this time. I looked around for any sign of movement or life, but there was none. It was just George and me. My mind told me that was impossible. I had many friends here in town, people from the Tim Hortons, the library, and even members of the town council or the business community. Where was everyone? The silence was deafening.

I decided to yell out, hoping someone would respond. But all I heard was the lonely howl of the wind. Not sure what came over me, I began to panic. I slid and skated my way back to my Humvee and decided to check several places around town that should have normally been filled with people by this time of day. Burning rubber and fishtailing in my panic, I went from one spot to another just to find the same things. They were all empty, and the only thing I heard was that deafening silence.

This can't be, I kept telling myself as I found more and more places empty. Then despair began to overtake me. My rational mind kept trying to come up with a rational solution to where all the people had gone. Then it came to me they must have evacuated the town due to the blackout. Yes, that was it' everyone had been taken to a central spot to keep warm. That would explain why the highway hadn't been cleared and why no one had answered the police phone at the dispatch center; only the dispatch center wasn't in Huntsville. But then, where had the people been taken? Not at the arena or the town community center or any other places normally used for such emergencies. Where then? And for how long?

After having checked a few more locations with the same results, no sign of life, I decided to go to the local airport where I keep two airplanes hangered over the winter months. In the summer, I used them as floatplanes. One was a PA-18 Piper Super Cub, which I left on floats. It was a two-seater that I use for short cargo runs or, sometimes, training new pilots for a float endorsement.

My other plane was a Cessna 185 Skywagon, which I would often use over the winter. Though it did come on floats, in the winter, I put wheeled landing gear on it. A larger aircraft, able to carry six people as well as several hundred pounds of cargo, the Skywagon was often referred to as the workhorse of bush flying. Its configuration was slightly different from many seen in the skies today, as its third wheel was at the back or tail of the plane. As mentioned, I used this plane over the winter for such things as transporting groceries or other supplies, as well as to be able to visit with family during the winter months. Our airport was a simple, single blacktop (tarred) runway with no control tower. As I had today become to expect, the runway was covered in ice and snow, but the salt truck was loaded and ready to go. I climbed into the cab. Having known the maintenance man, I knew where he hid the keys in the cab under the seat, and I started to salt the runway. It took four trips up and down the runway to clear away the ice and snow.

Once the runway was cleared of ice, I started my inspection of the Skywagon. I had little more than half fuel in the two wing tanks, which would get me to and from Toronto's Billy Bishop Airport on the lakefront where my son flew helicopters for the air ambulance service. I wanted to top up both tanks, but without power to run the pumps, I couldn't; I only hoped Toronto still had power.

My other concern was how much time everything was taking. It was already after two in the afternoon, and more storm clouds were threatening. The flight down to Toronto would be at least two hours, and sunset was around 5:00 p.m. I would likely be spending the night in Toronto. I grabbed a sandwich from the hangar cafeteria and gave George some no-name canned meat for his dinner and then loaded a couple of portable radios into my flight bag I kept at the airport, as well as the two handguns with three extra magazines for each.

Having been kept inside a hangar, the plane didn't need any deicing from the wings or fuselage. I opened the hangar doors with some difficulty, due to ice and snow cluttering up some of the runners. I started the engine. It took a couple of tries due to the cold. Then once it was running, I taxied right out to the runway and, seconds later, was Airborne.

CHAPTER 3

George was familiar with flying and would sit behind the front seats while we were on the ground and then lie down once, we were Airborne. As I went through the final preflight checklist, he watched over my shoulder. There were still patches of ice on the runway, and we could feel the tires slip and slide as our speed increased. Finally, the tail lifted off the ground, and a few seconds later, we were Airborne.

Due to the cloud cover, we were only able to get to 4,500 feet but that should have been enough that I could radio Toronto Air Traffic Control. That facility controlled all air traffic with in a 250-mile radius of Toronto. It was operated 24-7 and had its own power source should there be an interruption in power. It also could identify any aircraft by radar inside that radius.

As I leveled off at 4,500 feet, I radioed Toronto. "Toronto Air Traffic Control, this is Cessna 185, Golf Alpha Romeo Yankee" (GARY). "Over."

I waited thirty seconds but got no reply.

"Toronto Air Traffic Control, do you copy? Over," I repeated.

There was still no reply.

I then set my IFF radio to standby. An IFF radio is a transponder that talks directly to the radar computer system. I switched the IFF radio to transmit on frequency 1700 and then retransmitted my voice call to Toronto Air Traffic Control, telling them I was squawking on

1700 (squawking means to transmit a radio signal through the IFF to highlight your visibility on the radar screen) and again waited for a reply. This should have made my plane show up on their radar, pinpointing my location. But with no reply, I was lost as what else I could do.

This should not be happening. The eerie feeling of the deserted town was now compounded by the lack of contact with others from the outside world. Panic was again setting in as I navigated this unfamiliar territory. I repeated the radio call several times but still only got dead air.

I could feel my hands start to shake as I gripped the flight control wheel. I had never been in this position before—so alone. What should I do? George must have sensed something was wrong, as he put his head over my seat and rested it on my shoulder.

"Well, George, it looks like we have a big problem. Toronto isn't answering their radio, and there should be over a hundred planes in the air even if Toronto itself is closed."

That gave me another idea. Toronto may not be answering. But surely, somebody must be out there to answer my radio call. I radioed my intention to switch frequencies in case the problem might have been my reception and then began transmitting on the UNICOM (universal communications) channel. "PAN-PAN, PAN-PAN, PAN-PAN, this is Cessna 185 GARY." I gave my position and ended my transmission with, "Any station."

The term *PAN-PAN* is used to indicate an urgent message just short of declaring a *Mayday* distress call. Saying any station means that anyone hearing the transmission is to respond. This, however, seemed to also fall on deaf ears, as I still got no response, only dead radio air.

We were now about an hour out of Toronto's Billy Bishop Airport, named after World War I's greatest Allied flying ace, but would be entering possible flight paths of the jets taking off or landing at Toronto's main airport, Pearson. Even at 4,500 feet, this was restricted airspace, and the fines for unauthorized entry are substantial, but I had no choice. I made a slight course change to fly directly over the center of Pearson Airport to hopefully avoid any active runway.

After another fifteen minutes, I became aware of my engine sputtering and immediately began an engine failure checklist. First, checking my throttle settings, I engaged the engine preheat to eliminate any ice buildup in the carburetor and reset my fuel mixture (a setting to maximize the fuel to oxygen ratio). My two-wing tank fuel gauges were reading only about a quarter full each. I concluded there must be some other blockage in the fuel lines themselves. After I'd spent about five minutes going through all the checks, the engine died out completely, and I was left to glide the plane. At seventy knots of airspeed, I would be able to glide four feet forward for every foot of altitude. This gave me about three miles to find a suitable landing place. I was now well inside the city, so there wasn't much open space for a landing.

I issued a Mayday call over the radio but now didn't expect much of a response and began my preparations for a crash-landing. I turned off all electronics and the fuel pumps, set the trim to keep the plane at seventy knots, and harnessed George in the rear cargo department before getting back to the main controls. As I continued my unpowered descent, I found what appeared to be a multilane highway. Although at this time, it should have been rush hour, I was shocked to see this highway empty, with only a few cars off to the side and no hydro wires stretched across the lanes and decided it would be enough to land on.

The highway was still covered in ice, leaving my brakes mostly useless till one tire hit a clear patch, skidding the plane in a 270-degree circle; nearly flipping us over; and landing us in a snowbank, hard. I had gotten bounced around the plane's cabin a bit, hitting my head against the control panel and my shoulder against the inside of the door, but nothing appeared broken. My door appeared jammed against a snowbank and ice piled on the side of the highway, so I had to climb out the window on the other side of the plane. Before getting out, though, I released George from his harness and placed my flight bag containing the two radios and two handguns beside the window. Once outside, I inspected the plane and saw my tail gear was bent, as well as one of the blades of the propeller. There may also have been some bending of the fuselage, but that would need to be determined by a proper aircraft technician. The tail gear wouldn't really pose a problem. But the bent blade I would need to replace before I could fly the plane again. I silently hoped I would be able to find someone to help with that.

I knew from experience I was going to be sore in a couple of hours, so I told George we had to get on our way. I lifted him out of the plane and then grabbed my bag and took out the two handguns; the Desert Eagle I had in a holster, which I clipped onto my belt, and the Browning I put in the back of my pants. And we started walking down the deserted highway. I thought I knew the area a little and was near the East Mall. I figured that would be the best place to start looking for people. In the meantime, I tried to raise someone, anyone on the two portable radios but still got no response.

CHAPTER 4

I t was getting dark and cold, so I made the decision to look for people at the mall first. I was now getting sore from the banging around in the crash and hungry, having only had the sandwich I'd taken from the hangar earlier that day. The automatic doors remained shut as I attempted to enter the mall, and it was dark inside, but I was able to slide the doors open. "Just the power failure," I told George as we entered. The mall, like everywhere else, appeared to be deserted. The only sounds were George's paw nails scratching the tiled floor.

Being a Border collie, George has a strong instinct for herding. And this often showed itself by him trying to herd things such as kids on bikes, ducks, other dogs during free play, to name but a few. He would go into a crouch and lower his head before springing into action, barking and prancing left and right to try and bring his subject to the desired location. He could wait to pounce in that crouched position for several minutes, and nothing could take him off his intense attention on his subject till his prey was right in the spot for herding. I mention this just to explain what happened next as we approached the mall's food court.

With only the occasional emergency light working, the mall was in darkness. But my eyes soon adjusted to the dimness. As we approached the food court area, George went into his herding crouch in front of me, almost making me trip over him. I stopped and tried to see or hear what was making him go into that state. By his position, I knew it had to be something ahead of us, so I called out, "Hello. Is there anyone there?"

I got no answer, but George had begun a soft, deep-throated growl.

I unzipped my jacket to give me less restrictive access to my handguns and then called out again. "Is anyone there?" I slowly brought my hand around to the back of my pants and started to grip the handle of my Browning, my eyes darting left and right, trying to see any movement.

Suddenly, George was on his feet barking frantically, the fur on the back of his neck raised straight. I pulled the Browning out from my back and brought it to my front, giving way to a two-handed grip. "Who's there?" I yelled as my right thumb pulled back the hammer of my gun.

George continued to bark and prance around in front of me but keeping a distance between me and whatever was ahead of us. Finally, my eyes caught movement. It looked like people. They were moving toward me. Slowly, they approached but without a sound. I shouted for them to identify themselves, but they didn't. George was now barking frantically and keeping himself between them and myself. I warned them I was armed, but still they silently proceeded in my direction.

I leveled the Browning at the lead individual as I slowly began to retreat. There were now five people I could count in front of me. I suddenly heard another sound from behind me and took a quick look over my shoulder to see two more people approaching from my rear, less than ten meters away. As a quick reaction, I brought the Browning around and quickly fired off two rounds center of mass (this is where the police are trained to aim for at the center of the torso) of the closest person.

They kept coming. I must have been in shock. Those bullets didn't slow them at all. I shouted another warning and then fired two more shots, both of which connected with one of them. They just kept coming!

I circled to the group in front of me again and fired, hitting the first person. But still they just kept coming; this was impossible.

They were within five meters of me now when an irrational memory was triggered in my mind. It was crazy, but for some reason, I remembered my son years ago at an arcade telling me the only way to kill a zombie was with a headshot. I didn't believe in zombies, but my next shot was the person in front of me with a headshot. It went down, and I watched the brains splatter onto the floor. I blinked, not understanding what I'd just witnessed and in shock. But George attacked another one and bit into its leg, and I shot it in the head, causing it to go down. Then I turned and shot the two coming up from behind me in their heads; it took three rounds, but I got them both and returned my attention to the remaining three in front. I quickly emptied the Browning, and the shots echoed throughout the mall. But by the end, I had downed all targets.

They are just targets, I whispered to myself. *Just targets.*

I couldn't bring myself to think I had just killed seven people. Hunting animals was one thing. But killing people, as I'd learned from my time in the army, was something else entirely. There was something else strange about these targets—their smell. Though I had just shot them, they had the reek of death a few days or more old. I decided to investigate further, and on inspection, I found I had indeed hit my mark with every round. So it appeared the only way to stop them was with the headshot.

Both George and I had gotten out of the scuffle unscathed. But night was just beginning, and I was already down one magazine of ammunition. That left me with thirty-nine rounds of 9mm for the Browning and thirty-two rounds for the Desert Eagle. I had no idea how many of these creatures there were. But in a city of over four million people, I was certain I had an extremely limited chance of killing them all. Despite having come to the food court to eat, I found myself no longer hungry. I instead grabbed some bottles of juice and some sport bars for later and organized what resources I had left.

Feeling I had taken care of my nutrition situation, I then went to my next concern, which was a toss-up between shelter and ammunition. Being inside a mall gave me shelter, but I had to wonder if there were more zombies lurking about. I thought about how I could use a part of the mall to build a defensive position.

The most important thing to remember when planning a defensive position is to have an escape route. That always seemed to be the problem in the movies. People would barricade themselves into a spot. But when the barricade was breached, and it always was, they had no way to get out. I decided not to get into that situation, seeing as I had such a limited amount of ammunition and an unknown number of enemies. The numbers didn't look to be in my favor.

CHAPTER 5

The search for ammunition, I decided, would be my next priority. This was going to be more of a problem, however, because Toronto, unlike many American cities, didn't have a gun shop on every corner; and finding pistol ammunition was even rarer. We did have a good supply of sporting goods stores that carried the likes of golf clubs and running shoes, but very few stores in the big city would carry actual hunting supplies. If memory served me right, there was a specialty store nearby. I decided to head in that direction to find out.

It turned out I was right. There was a sporting goods store just a few blocks away called Sail, and I knew it carried hunting supplies. Whether it would carry any handgun ammo would be another matter, but it did have hunting rifles. I kept close to the buildings just to keep a low profile. When we got to the store, I found the doors locked. I hesitated to break the glass doors, as it would make a lot of noise, and I wanted the doors to be able to stop any zombie attack. I quietly followed the building around to the back loading docks, where I found one door slightly ajar. It led to the shipping and receiving office kept open by a pack of cigarettes. I slowly opened the door and crouched down, peering inside the darkened store. George, standing beside me, gave no indication there was any danger, so I duckwalked into the storage area. Once inside, I stood with my back firmly against the wall. Holding my breath, I waited for my eyes to adjust to the darkness again. I pulled the Browning from the back of my pants and pointed it straight ahead of me at waist height for a possible torso shot.

I had a penlight, which I now turned on and held in my left hand and cupped it along the barrel of my gun to see what was in the direction the gun was facing. Holding both the pen-light and Browning, I brought both hands stretched out in front of me at shoulder height, penlight in left and pistol in right, as George and I began to explore the inside. After the first few steps, I turned and locked the door behind me to not have any surprises. Then we continued exploring the store. The loading area was about fifteen meters by forty-five meters and, as expected, there were many flats holding product for sale all around the floor. These made perfect hiding places for me but also for zombies that might be here in the store. It would take all night to check the entire area, and we'd still have no assurance that we hadn't missed something. So, I decided to forgo that search and just barricade the doors once we were on the shopping floor.

I came out of the loading zone into the camping supplies area. I shone my flashlight around several aisles and saw no signs movement. George had stayed by my side up to this point and then broke away to explore an aisle on his own ahead of me. I figured, if he felt safe, I could relax a bit. Scanning what was on the shelves as we explored, I stopped as an item grabbed my attention. I took it off the shelve, and it felt heavy. As I opened the box, I found it contained ball bearings. I grabbed several more boxes and walked to the end of the aisle where I emptied two boxes onto the floor. I did the same thing for a couple more aisles. I figured the ball bearings would trip up anyone stepping on them and create enough noise to alert me to their presence. I just had to remember which aisles I'd put them down so I wouldn't also be caught in my own trap. I had also come across some glow sticks, which I could use as a light source. I used some of these to light the aisles I had not booby-trapped.

The floor plans were terribly similar to the many other box stores now ubiquitous here, making it easier for the customer to find items, as well as enabling employees from one store to transfer to another without major retraining. The hunting and fishing departments in Sails were always connected on the upper floor. Being in the camping section, I was able to find other important necessities, such as sleeping bags, cooking utensils, and dehydrated foods. With the glow stick in my hand, I checked the shelves and then walked up the stairs to the fishing and hunting supplies.

It had grown dark and very cold outside, and with no power, the building began to feel like a refrigerator. Upstairs, I began to look for the keys to the gun cabinets but couldn't find any. I tried to pull some guns off the shelve, but that wasn't going to happen. Gun safety was taken very seriously here. Finally, I found a crossbow and about twenty arrows for it.

I went back downstairs to see if I could find any keys but to no avail. However, I did come across a crowbar, which I took back upstairs with me. I also came across a newspaper, which I took, figuring I'd read it later. It took me ten more minutes to break the locking system to some of the guns and ammunition. I now had six rifles to augment my handguns, including a thirty ought six with a low light scope. I loaded each weapon to their max and then loaded as many extra magazines as I could find.

I started up a portable stove I got from the camping section to heat some water and make some dinner, took up position to observe anyone approaching the stairs, wrapped myself in a sleeping bag for warmth, and then began to read the newspaper. There in large bold print was the headline:

North Korean Subs Launch Missile Attacks On North American Cities

North Korea didn't wait to complete its testing of its ICBMs that could reach mainland US of A. Instead, they launched medium-range missiles from two submarines located off the coast in both the Pacific and the Atlantic oceans. The two subs were positioned just over 200 kilometers from shore and were able to launch nine missiles before being destroyed. The sneak attack came in response to the American president's demand for North Korea to stop its continued testing of long-range missiles and nuclear weapons or face military intervention.

The missiles, which didn't carry any nuclear warheads, struck cities—Los Angles (two missiles); San Francisco; Seattle; Washington, DC; Boston; New York (two missiles); and Toronto, Canada.

Initial damage was thought to be minimal, with Toronto's death toll being estimated at between 800 and 1,000 people. However, with in fifteen minutes of the attack, first responders and other survivors seemed to be just dropping dead. With the help of the CDC in Atlanta and Homeland security, it was discovered the warheads had been a chemical compound like the nerve agent Anthrax. Within an hour of the initial blast, Toronto's death toll rose to over 10,000, and a hot zone of 5 kilometers was set up from the blast site.

The problems didn't end there either. Janice Smith, a nurse at Sunny Brook Hospital, claimed that as she and other hospital workers were bringing in bodies for the makeshift morgue, several reanimated. There have also been several other such reports of dead coming back to life and attacking the living. The situation got so bad the city of Toronto was ordered evacuated.

There were few reports coming out of the American cities also targeted at the time of printing.

The newspaper was from Hamilton and dated six days ago. At first, I thought it must be a gag paper, a joke like you can get at the CNE. I didn't want to believe it; I couldn't believe it. Then the pieces of the puzzle began to take shape—what I had seen on the video and was going to report, the town of Huntsville empty, no one at Toronto Air Traffic Control, the highway with no moving traffic at rush hour, and those things coming at George and me inside the mall. It was too much for me. What had the world done? What had we done to the world?

Going into despair, I went into deep contemplation. What had happened to my family? Where were my children? Though they were adults now and living their own lives, they were still my children! My son flew rescue helicopters, and my daughter was a hospital administrator. Their respective careers would put them both on the front lines of this disaster. That realization brought me back to the here and now. I pulled out the radio sets I had and again tried to transmit a Mayday, first on the aviation radio then on the CB.

I was still getting nothing back but dead air. "What the hell happened, George? Where are they?" I asked George as he lay at my feet.

Then there was a sound from outside like a howling that made George and me get to our feet. There were a few windows here on the second level, so I crept up to one to peer out. Though it was dark outside, it wasn't pitch-black. And soon, I was able to make out some movement. I told George to keep quiet while I ran back to one of the aisles. I was looking for some binoculars labeled "night vison" on the box. I would use them to spy down from the window once more. They were low light as opposed to inferred, which would require a heat source. Considering the heat source hadn't worked for the creatures on the trail cams, I guessed the low light would be better to observe with.

It wasn't as good as I had hoped. But it did let me make out several human forms walking slowly outside moving in the same slow style as those in the mall had earlier. Snapping my fingers to draw George's attention, I gave him a hand signal he knew meant to be still and quiet. So, he adopted his crouch till I gave all clear.

At first, the zombies appeared to be a small group, but within minutes, their numbers rapidly increased. If I had to guess, I would say they soon numbered over a hundred. Perhaps a dozen or so I could handle but not a hundred. Thus far, they didn't seem to know of my whereabouts, so we just continued to hide quietly in the upstairs of the Sail store.

George and I had a fretful sleep for the second night in a row. I was cold, tired, and stiff from the hard landing. I tried the radios several times throughout the night but always with the same results. I now had several decisions to make with limited information. Should I continue to Billy Bishop Airport and hope to find my son? I knew now that the city had been evacuated. But would he maybe still be there helping rescue people? Where had the evacuees gone?

Or should I just head back home again? Could I do something to help here?

Then I began to consider some of the bigger questions on my mind, like what had happened to the world since the attacks? Surely the Americans would have retaliated, although one of the cities hit had been Washington, DC. Had the president been killed? What would the retaliation have been? A nuclear strike? Under normal circumstances, I would think not. But this president was very unpredictable. And I also had to consider that not only was this a sneak attack, it had also been one using chemical weapons, something outlawed by every civilized country in the world. What if this had something to do with North Korea? Would China be willing to support its trading partner after the use of chemical weapons? And if China joined the mix, would Russia be far behind? Russia was still a giant when it came down to nuclear arsenals. Things could rapidly go the way of the domino effect—each action being met with a stronger reaction.

I had all the questions but none of the answers. The newspaper was almost a week old. Could World War III have been fought in less than a week? The answer appeared to be a resounding *yes*! I began to review the facts as I knew them. First, I hadn't seen a living person since coming to Toronto. Second, I'd had no success contacting people over the radio. Granted, CB radio was no longer as popular as it once was and my aviation radio even less so. But still, absolutely no contact wasn't reasonable. Internet service was out, mainly due to the power outage. But was the power outage because we no longer had people to man it?

As daylight was dawning and the glow sticks, I had used the night before were losing their illumination inside the store, I had to decide what to do. I could stay in the building. There was lots of canned food and lots of ammunition. But really, one man could only fire one gun at a time accurately. What would staying do for me? I was already starting to think of the ghosts of shoppers who, only a week ago, had carried on with their lives, asking the salesperson stupid questions about canoeing or running or some other trivial matter. It was, frankly, an eerie feeling and one I wasn't comfortable with. It was a condition known as survivor's guilt.

CHAPTER 6

H aving snuck the occasional peek through the upper floor windows and seen more zombies than I could possibly count throughout the night, I noticed their numbers appeared to dwindle during the day to maybe in the dozens. This suggested the best time to travel would be during the daylight hours. I didn't know if it meant they rested, if zombies rest, during the day or if they disliked the sunlight. With their gray complexions, that was a possibility. These questions weren't my concern. My concern was what I would do now. And where would I go?

With the city having been evacuated and the fact that I had continued to fail in all my attempts to get radio communication with anyone, it no longer made sense to continue my trip to Billy Bishop. I seemed alone. All these thoughts were running through my mind as I made and ate a breakfast of dehydrated bacon and eggs with a cup of instant black coffee with no sugar. I was usually a Triple/Triple kind of guy.

Well, since there appeared to be fewer zombies walking around during the day, then that would be my time to travel. But to where I hadn't decided. Even during the day, I would need a clear path of escape. That would mean shooting my guns. Would the gunshots draw too much attention? Did zombies respond to noise, especially the loud reports of gunfire? Could they warn others of my escape route to block me in, if by nothing else, just sheer numbers? Did they communicate with each other and how?

White-tailed deer would hear a gunshot from over a mile away and, raising their tails so to expose the white underside, warn other animals of the presence of danger. Did the zombies have a system of communication?

As I worked on a second cup of coffee, wishing for some cream and sugar, I began to revisit my memory of the confrontation the night before. The zombies appeared to move very slowly, and they hadn't seemed to react to the loud reports of the gunfire. Although a 9mm round was in no way near as loud as, say, a shotgun blast, in the food court, it should have been considered very loud. And the zombies hadn't seemed to care those members of their group had had their brains blown all over the floors. Was this a lack of empathy or remorse for their fellow zombies? Or was it because they were totally focused on their one goal, getting to me? Or perhaps they were just mindless eating machines? Five had come at me from the front, but also two had come up from behind. Was this their effort to trap me? Or was it just a coincidence—two separate groups acting independently of each other? It seemed more prudent not to accept anything as a coincidence for the time being.

I decided I could remain in the Sail store for a day or two. I then used a forklift to place flats of material against the loading doors, hoping to safeguard against a breech. The door I had used for my entry was now closed and locked. Though it seemed secure, I placed some heavy boxes up against it just to be safe. The front doors I blocked with a few more heavy boxes and canoes. As I was moving things around, I found some stairs in the back of the second level that seemed to go to the roof. I would check on them later. The windows I had been using to peek through the night before were sealed and could not be opened. I tried to break one, first with the butt of the Browning and then with the butt of one of the 12-gauge shotguns, but the windows held firm. I was of a mixed opinion to congratulate the company on their security or tear someone's throat out with frustration.

I wisely decided to leave the matter alone and, instead, went to explore the stairs I had found earlier. The stairs were behind a wall between the stock and showroom and led up to a door at the top. I could see the door from where I stood and proceeded up to investigate. What first concerned me was the sign on the door saying, "Alarm will sound if opened." Should I take the risk? With no power for several days now and only a limited amount of backup, power was likely gone. I took a deep breath and pushed against the bar, opening the door, and heard nothing. With no alarm, I began to breathe again. Slowly, I inched the door open with my Browning drawn and pointed ahead of me. As I slowly shuffled through the door, I found a piece of a two-by-four and several cigarette butts scattered around. I had found the staff's smoking corner.

Propping the door open with my knapsack, I crept around the roof, keeping as low a profile as I could. There were some high-rise buildings all around me, and though I didn't think they were occupied by zombies, I did have to ask myself who might still be occupying them. And did I want them to know where I was with food, water, and weapons? Were we in a fight for survival of the fittest? The roof was slippery with ice and water as the sun now shone and warmed the air, so I lay on my belly and crawled to the roof's edge. I was able to see most of the street below and figured there were three or four dozen zombies wandering about. I followed the edge all around the building to see if there would be fewer zombies around the back. I counted only about a dozen in and around the rear loading area. The numbers were suggesting that would be my better escape route, but I decided I needed more information to develop a proper plan.

I crawled and scooted on all fours back to the door and inside. The front of my clothes was soaked with ice cold water, so I went to the clothing section and got a change of dry clothes.

While changing clothes, I began developing my plan. It involved eliminating the threat from the rear of the building, which I had established to be my line of least resistance. I grabbed the thirty ought six and two extra magazines. This would give me a total of eighteen rounds. I still wasn't sure if the sound of the gunfire would attract them, so I got several items to make a silencer for the rifle. The term "silencer" is actually a misnomer; it doesn't silence the gun but rather muffles the sound, like a muffler on a car. Of course, silencers are also illegal in Canada, so you can't just go to a sporting store and buy one. But there are several items you can use to make a homemade one, and that was what I did. It was crude and would likely mess up some of the accuracy of the rifle, but you had to do what you had to do.

Once I had secured the silencer onto the gun, I got the extra magazines and a four-foot-by-eight-foot ground sheet and went back out onto the roof. I then changed into some hip waders and a raincoat that could be tied tightly at the waist. I slowly crawled to about four feet from the edge, just enough to look over and see most of the outside loading area. I spread out the ground sheet so just a couple of inches hung over the edge and then slowly edged my way to the ledge, assuming a prone position.

At first glance over the edge, I saw eight people I took to be zombies. *Damn*, I thought. I would need to change magazines to get them all. I placed the two extra magazines down on the ground sheet to my left for easy reach and then pressed the magazine release button and reinserted the magazine several times to ensure smooth motion. I then swung the barrel over the edge and began to take aim. My first target was the closest at forty meters. It would have been an easy shot even without the scope; however, it was important that I make a headshot. The head is only one-sixth the area of the torso, and I had a newly homemade silencer on the barrel, which could affect my aim and shot.

I raised my head to check around one last time and returned my attention to the target in my scope. I slowed my breathing, released the safety, and placed my target's head in my crosshairs. Slowly I squeezed the trigger till I felt the recoil and heard a modest *pop*. Without even following through on the shot, I rolled over onto my back and brought the gun prone to my side. I was breathing rapidly, thinking, *Did they see me? Do they know where I am now?*

Though the sound had been softened by the silencer, was it enough to avoid being noticed? Had I even hit my target?

I had to tell myself to control my breathing, but this wasn't a normal hunting situation. I was now hunting people. No! Not people. These creatures were predators, and I had to kill or risk being killed. It took a minute, but the fear and revulsion subsided, and I began to think normally again. I slowly peered over the edge and, to my surprise, found my target lying on the ground with blood pooling around its head. Headshot! And none of the other zombies seemed to notice.

I quietly ejected the spent casing and chambered my next round. My next target was about fifty-five meters. I scanned the area again to see if I was drawing any unwanted attention and then scoped my target. Again, I squeezed the trigger, felt the kick of the rifle, and heard a slightly louder *pop*. This time, I stayed and watched as the projectile hit its mark, splattering skull and gray matter over a dumpster. Still no response from the others. Same thing happened for the third and fourth targets. My only concern was that each shot seemed to be louder than the last.

The muzzle flash appeared to have ignited the steel wool I had used to muffle the sound, and by the fourth round, it had started burning. I had to pull the silencer off the barrel with my left hand, receiving a sore but mild burn. Some of the tape I had used to secure it in place still stuck to the barrel, making the can dangle in the breeze. I retrieved all the magazines but left the ground sheet in place and crawled back to the door. Once inside, I tore the can from the barrel and went downstairs to make another silencer.

It took me all of fifteen minutes to install a new silencer and return to the roof again, crawling to the edge and on the ground sheet. When I looked over the edge, I got a big rude surprise. Instead of only the four remaining zombies, there were now a dozen in the alleyway. How had they known I was clearing a path? Or was this just another coincidence? They didn't seem concerned about those I had shot. I figured I had no other choice but to continue clearing the path for escape, so I took up my firing position again and started shooting.

Again, the zombies didn't appear to take any notice of the gunfire or the dropping of their fellow zombies one after the other with their heads splattering from each high-velocity impact. In under fifteen minutes, there were now sixteen dead zombies throughout the alleyway. I then waited and watched. After about twenty minutes, a new zombie showed up and then a couple more a few minutes after that. Then they started showing up in small groups of three or four.

Ninety minutes after I had fired my first shot, the alley was filled with over thirty zombies. I figured I wasn't going to be able to use that exit today. I was forced to consider spending another night in the store.

fter George and I had another meal of dehydrated food, we inspected the store again, paying special attention to possible entry points for the zombies, as well as exit strategies for escape for the two of us. I made an executive decision that the upstairs was still our safest location, as it provided only one way up and an exit to the roof. The only problem with that was how we would get back down if we got stuck on the roof. I supposed I could climb down, but George would be another problem; under no circumstances was I going to leave George behind.

Yet another night approached, and the streets began to fill with zombies. We stood on the roof watching as they spilled onto the streets of Toronto in the hundreds. I had brought both radios with me, as well as two of the rifles I had commandeered. Once again, I had the thirty ought six but also a .22 caliber semiautomatic with a ten-round magazine. I had tied George up to the roof door to ensure he wouldn't slip over the edge of the building. Then while on my hands and knees, I approached the sides to see what was happening.

To my southwest, I caught some unusual movement. It was somebody running. Then I heard the hollow popping sounds of gunfire and saw two of the zombies closest to the person hit the ground; however, a dozen others seemed to quickly replace them. I unswung the .22 from around my body and then raised the thirty-ought-six with its scope to my shoulder, taking careful aim at the attacking zombies. It was over five hundred meters away, and even with the scope, the shot was going to be difficult, especially for a headshot; the body would have been easier.

My first shot was about center of the lead zombie's back, and though the hit did seem to slow it down slightly, it continued its advance on the runner. I chambered a second round and quickly drew a bead on the same zombie but this time trying for a headshot. The head being a small moving target at that range, I missed. Chambering my third round and having cursed myself, I took an extra moment to calm my breathing; sighted the zombie; and shot, this time taking off the left side of his head and dropping him.

I then quickly chambered another round and, sighting the next lead zombie, hit him in the head. I was able to stop four more zombies before they captured their quarry. And the result was preordained with sheer numbers; the zombies began to rip their victim to shreds. I had a momentary flashback to what I had seen on the trail cam, which had started me on this journey. I sat at the edge of the roof mortified but could not help this poor runner.

Instead, I loaded my next magazine and began to fire on the mob of zombies as they devoured their kill. Once I had exhausted all the thirty-ought-six rounds, I had brought with me to the roof, I then started to fire down on the packs of zombies with the .22. It was not nearly strong enough to kill them at 500 meters but was quick, being a semiauto and good for killing closer zombies, at a range of about 150 meters. By the end of that twenty minutes of action, I had spent more than a hundred rounds of ammunition and had dropped between thirty-five and fifty zombies, but there were still thousands more out there.

I no longer worried about the sounds of my gunfire. I just wanted to kill all the zombies I could now. With no scope and much less power, I had taken out closer targets. But with the .22, the bullet would hit the head but not go all the way through the skull like the thirty-ought-six, so I couldn't always be sure I had a proper hit. However, with the lighter kickback and the semiauto configuration, I found I could fire off the ten-round mag with seven or eight head hits inside of thirteen seconds. The one major discovery from this battle was that there were survivors, and they were hiding here in the city.

I suppose that gave me some hope that I would be able to find my family. I had brought both radios with me up to the rooftop and now tried to send out a signal, first with the UHF radio used by aircraft; when that still didn't work, I tried the CB radio.

I was about to give up when I heard what sounded like a garbled transmission. It was a very weak signal, and I tried several times to respond to it. But it appeared I was either out of range or being blocked by the height of the surrounding buildings. To counter this shortfall, emergency services such as police, fire, and ambulance, as well as some taxi companies went to satellite service; it gave a better line of sight and wasn't interfered with by tall structures and obstacles. So that combined with my weaker signal prevented me from establishing contact with whoever was sending that call out over their radio. But at least I knew they were out there, and by circling my antenna, I was able to determine a very general direction where the signal was coming from. I had already decided to spend another night in the store. But now I had an idea of which direction to head when I tried to leave the next morning.

Though we had enough food and protection to last for several days or weeks even, especially now having knowledge the city hadn't been entirely abandoned and there were still some people around, I was ready to go. I wanted to make early contact just to have somebody to talk to. But as the evening progressed, I began to question whether that was really such a good idea. Who would be left behind? And why? I had food, weapons, and ammunition. These possessions would be ripe for the taking by an undesirable element of society, but shared, they could be the difference between life and death or even just survival.

I returned to the cabinets containing the remainder of the guns and finally broke it open. I then packed all the guns and food I could find into a canoe I had placed by a side loading door. I guessed this made the canoe weigh some five hundred pounds. I was able to open the door quietly and slip out, and then I dragged the canoe out with me. I hid it along the side of the building, thinking that the zombies didn't seem interested in anything they couldn't eat. Then I returned to the store and George, as he was standing there waiting for me. In the morning, I figured, George and I would be able to slide the canoe over the ice and snow just like a sled. It was better than leaving so many useful items behind. At the very least I had items, I could barter and trade when the time came. I just hoped I was right, and the zombies wouldn't bother with the canoe and its contents overnight.

I used another set of glow stick to light up the store for the night and set up our sleeping location upstairs on the upper level, again blocking off the stairs with boxes, canoes, and kayaks. I used a blow-up mattress and a cold-weather sleeping bag to sleep in after the dark streets again seemed to swarm with zombies. I was out cold from sheer exhaustion within minutes of cuddling up in the warm sleeping bag.

I was awakened by George as he began to give a low growl. But still being half-asleep, I told him to relax and lie down. Then there was the crash of breaking glass, and George began barking, sending the adrenalin through my system, and bringing me to full awareness. I struggled to get out of the sleeping bag while trying to calm George. Finally, after what seemed an eternity but in reality, was only a few seconds, I was out of the sleeping bag and spied over the railing to see what was happening. Through the glow of my lighting system, I could observe several slow-moving figures entering the store. George, standing at the top of the stairs, growled, and barked at the intruders.

I grabbed the closest rifle near me, which was a Winchester 94 (a lever action .30-30 caliber rifle), checked that a bullet was in the chamber, cocked back the hammer, and began to take aim. More zombies appeared to be coming through the now broken glass doors, and some seemed to be heading straight for the stairs, George, and me. Several started down the aisles I had booby-trapped with the ball bearings, and they went flying onto their backs as their feet went out from under them. More followed and found the way impassable. But by sheer numbers, they began to pile onto each other, climbing over one another. This left only two aisles I had left clear for them to come at us and gave me truly clear shots at them.

As the first zombie found the clear aisle, I took aim and began to fire. It was like shooting fish in a barrel. The only problem was, for each zombie I shot, it seemed two would take its place. I had plenty of ammunition. But as the hammer hit an empty chamber, I realized the time it would take to reload. Unlike the thirty-ought-six or the .22 with magazine clips that could be replaced in a matter of seconds, the Winchester 94 used a tube, and to reload that would take about half a minute—but that could be a lifetime. Therefore, I grabbed the next nearest gun, which was a Remington—34-inch 12-gauge pump-action shotgun.

Several of the zombies were now about ten meters from the stairs. I again took up a firing position, firing down onto them. With the closeness of the shots, I was literally obliterating their heads and faces as they disintegrated under the force of the shot pellets. After five more shots, the Remington was also empty. And now, some of the zombies had regained their footing from the aisles with the ball bearings. I knew I wouldn't be able to get all of them as they got through the early defenses; I grabbed the next loaded rifle.

also spied a hurricane lamp I had filled earlier nearby. I picked it up and sloshed it about, confirming it still held fuel. As the zombies were now at the barrier I had put up at the bottom of the stairs, I lit the wick and, with all the force I could muster, threw the lamp at the base of the stairs. It exploded in a whoosh of flame, engulfing that side of the stairs as well as several zombies. They appeared to walk away looking like human torches. But after a few steps, they just dropped as their flesh melted away. Seems I had discovered another method of killing them. However, the spreading fire also blocked one possible escape route for us.

The fire, however, did give me time to reload the two guns I had been using. And again I was able to concentrate on one area of attack. I began shooting down into the zombies. They now avoiding coming through the flames for the most part, but a couple did get a bit too close to the flames and lit up like Roman candles.

After thirty minutes, the store was filling with the strong odor of burning and decayed flesh, with approximately ninety to a hundred zombies scattered or bunched on the store's main floor. There were still some stragglers coming through the broken glass in the front of the store, but I had plenty of time to take them out safely from the upper level. The fire, in the meantime, had spread to some items down several aisles but seemed to burn itself out.

After such an adrenalin rush and the apparent calm that followed, along with the fire having used up so much oxygen, I found myself getting dozy and nodded off several times. The exhaustion began to overtake me, and I found it difficult to stay alert.

At about 5:30 in the morning, I was once again startled awake by George's sharp barks of warning. At first, I was sore and stiff. Then I peered over the edge of the railing only to view ten new zombies who had silently gained entry to the store.

I immediately grabbed for a rifle and started shooting. I got six with seven shots, but more were pouring through the doorways. I knew just by the numbers coming in I wouldn't be able to hold them all off for long. Having to step over or around those I had already killed slowed them down but didn't deter them from progressing on my location.

I lit three more hurricane lamps and threw them smashing into the aisles, blocking them with fire. One of the aisles had camping fuel for the stoves, which began several small explosions and intensified the fire that, this time, was spreading out of control through the store. The smoke and heat were choking, but still the zombies continued their advance toward George and me. A number had finally reached the barricade at the bottom of the stairs despite all my efforts to stop them.

I quickly blocked off the top of the stairs. I got George, and we headed to the stairs to the roof and the door outside. I had used up the ammunition for the Winchester and shotgun, so I left them behind and drew my pistol. I also grabbed rope and a doggy life vest and threw these out the door. I then lit my last lantern and, from the doorway at the top of the stairs, threw it down, setting the stairwell on fire to prevent the zombies from coming up it. Unfortunately, that also cut off our likely escape route.

Once out on the roof, I used anything I could find to block the door. We listened as the roar of the fire engulfed the store with several more explosions going off, presumably small propane tanks. Though it was still dark, I could see the sun just below the horizon to the east. I went to the edge of the roof and was able to see the back of the store was mostly cleared of zombies. So I decided to go with my original plan from the day before and use this back route for escape. I had more than enough experience and rope to repel down the side of the building, but the problem was how to get George down. I grabbed the pet life preserver I had taken and secured it snuggly on George. I looped one end of the rope through the handle, making sure the knots were well secured.

Finding a location near the rear edge of the building, I gently lifted George and began to lower him down. George at first didn't like the fact he wasn't able to touch any surface with his all fours and began to squirm, pulling me off balance. But I was able to calm him talking to him as I lowered him to the ground some thirty meters below. The roof was now smoking and bubbling, so I knew I had a truly short time to get off that roof as the fire raged below. I tried looking for a secure spot to fasten the rope while I repelled down but didn't see anything good so ended up fastening it to the doorknob and just hoped it would hold my weight. Flames had started coming through the roof, so I had no more time to test anything, and over the side I went, near where I had lowered George. He started barking as he watched me repel down the side of the building and I had to give him a hand signal to stay where he was and be quiet till I finished climbing down. Once on the ground, I quickly removed the improvised harnesses from both of us.

Sticking close to the side of the building, I went around the front just enough to see the street in front of the store. Flames now engulfed the entire inside of the structure, and I could see through the reflection that the street was heavily populated with what I assumed were zombies. Well, we were going to have to find somewhere else for shelter. I went back to the rear of the building, where I had left the canoe filled with guns, food, and ammunition earlier that night. I pulled it away from the burning building but was too tired to take it far so left it hidden behind a trailer while George and I found a new hopefully safe place to get some sleep.

CHAPTER 9

We found another box store, a hardware center, that had several sheds built so we ducked into a wooden one and opened a glow stick. It was bitterly cold in the predawn, but at least we were out of sight. I lay down on the raised wooden floor while George rested his upper half of his body over my chest to share our bodies' heat. Sometime later, I was able to doze to another fitful sleep. In that sleep state, my mind began putting some pieces of the puzzle together. First there was the attack in the mall from two different directions. Then there was my shooting zombies in the back alley behind the store. It had started out with only eight, but when I'd taken the time to build a new silencer and come back, they had increased in number. And then you look at this last night. On my first night, they left the store alone; but after I had shot those zombies during the day, they'd attacked the store—and in large numbers. This was suggesting that they did somehow communicate and had the ability to at least semi-plan their actions. They weren't just murderous, killing machines. This brewed up a vastly different kettle of fish.

I awoke that morning cold and even more stiff than before, but the sun was shining through the small window of the shed. I got stiffly to my feet and tried hard to listen for any movement of zombies outside. All was unnaturally quiet. My watch told me it was going on to nine o'clock in the morning. And in a city the size of Toronto, there should be the sounds of traffic and people going about their business. But the only sound I could hear was the whining of the wind blowing through the cracks in the shed's walls and up the wooden floor. The weather seemed to be warming, but I was still chilled deep down in my bones. I knew I had to find warmth quickly before hypothermia set in. I could already feel its onset.

Inching the door to the shed slowly open, I peered out, looking for any zombies. The shed door began to squeak as I opened it wider. It was incredibly soft, but to me it sounded like a loud clap of thunder, and I froze in mid opening. It was George, who just zipped past me, knocking the door wide open. He then turned to face me with his tail wagging and gave a soft bark, followed by two more sharp barks, twisting his head around as to make sure no one else was nearby. I pulled out my Desert Eagle from its holster and then cautiously joined him in the warming glow of the sun.

We crossed back over to the trailer where I had hidden the canoe with all our supplies and found it as we had left it. Meanwhile, parts of the Sail store continued to burn, filling the air with smoke and the smell of burning dead flesh. I figured I now knew what it must have been like to live near the Nazis' death camps during World War II. I had to choke back vomit. The smoke itself wasn't too bad. But as I said, it was the stench of the burning zombies that hung in the air that made the area unbearable. I quickly decided it was time for us to leave.

I had made a sort of harness from a hunting vest and rope I had taken from the store and used that to allow me to pull the canoe over the ice and snow behind me. It had been a good idea till today's temperature began to get warmer and started to melt the ice. Holstering my Desert Eagle, I slung another shotgun over my shoulder and carried the thirty-ought-six. Then with three meters of rope, I began to pull the canoe, trailing it behind me; George and I had to head out. But which way to head out to? The highway I had crash-landed on was to my east. Billy Bishop Airport was to my southeast. And the radio signal I had gotten the day before was also to my east, so that was the direction we headed in.

It was slow going dragging some five hundred pounds of supplies in the canoe and trying to stay close to buildings to be able to hide should the need arise. I tried on several occasions to get a response from whoever I'd heard on the CB radio. But the cold from the night before had drained the batteries, giving even less range, till they died out completely.

Traveling east, I figured the first thing to do was return to the plane to have a closer look at the damage and see what I could do to repair it. Shock and low visibility had likely hampered my first inspection. Now with the fullness of bright daylight, I could do a more proper inspection. I found the plane still on the highway where I had left it a few days ago. Not sure why I should have been surprised; it wasn't like someone could just come and take it.

A few days ago, I couldn't believe all that had happened in just a few days. It all seemed like a blur. I had gone out to check the cameras for the trails and then found myself in a ghost town of Toronto. As I approached the plane at first glance, it didn't appear that severely damaged. The snowbank it had ended up in had been melting, so not nearly as deeply buried as first appeared. One blade of the propeller was seriously bent and would need to be replaced, and the tail gear appeared bent as well. But it was still operational. The fiberglass tip of the port wing was crushed, but that didn't have any effect on the ailerons or the flaps. It was one of the reasons they were so popular for bush flying; often could still be flown after a crash with a minimum amount of repair and these planes were made sturdy. The fuel tanks were almost empty though, so I was going to need to get some avgas, but from where and how? And where would I go even if I got the plane going again? I had to stop thinking like that. I had to remain positive. I had seen and heard signs of people out there. I just needed to find them.

I loaded about two-thirds of my supplies into the cargo hold of the 185, making the canoe much lighter, found some fresh batteries for the CB radio, harnessed up again, and told George we were off to Billy Bishop. The day was warming up as I walked down that lonely, barren highway. But as there had been no snow removal or clearing, it allowed the canoe to just float over the ground. When we got to one of the exit ramps near the lake, we then headed east again toward the downtown. Being back onto residential streets, I was struck with an overwhelming sense of loneliness.

George and I tried to stay close to the buildings and homes to stay as out of sight as possible. On several occasions, we would need to backtrack and change our route as we would come across bands of zombies. George was exceptionally good at sensing them out and warning me. I can only assume it was his high sense of smell and their rotting flesh that gave them away. They seemed to shuffle very quietly. When George knew some were nearby, he would go into his crouch and give a low growl of warning. We hoped they wouldn't hear us, and it seemed we were in luck, as we seemed to succeed in keeping away from them.

With the fresh batteries for the CB radio, I would stop every half hour or so and turn it on to monitor for any transmissions. I had decided it would be safer for me not to do any transmissions till I could identify who was also transmitting. Then with all our stops and detours and the slow pace from dragging the canoe, we finally arrived at the pedestrian tunnel leading to Billy Bishop Airport. The airport itself was on an island out in Lake Ontario and was only reachable by ferry. That had finally changed near the turn of the century with the building of a tunnel to connect the island airport only to the mainland. The tunnel was at the foot of Bathurst Street with the entrance in the old Tip Top Tailors factory, which had been declared a historic site. The tunnel went some 25 meters deep under the channel from the mainland to the island. It was only about 270 meters long but now pitch-dark due to there being no electricity for the lighting.

Having recovered some food, a sleeping bag, three rifles, and over a hundred rounds of ammunition, I hid the canoe in some bushes beside the building. I then very slowly journeyed down the tunnel using a headlamp flashlight I had taken for the Sail's store to keep my hands free. Through the deep, dark tunnel, the only sounds were our footsteps on the tiled floor. As I walked along, I also deposited glow sticks to be able to see any approach of zombies from behind.

Once on the other side of the tunnel, we found exactly what we expected, what we had been finding all along in this city of over four million—no one, not a soul, just the same quiet as prevailed throughout the city. I wasn't really surprised, but I was disappointed. My son's air ambulance station was there, so I guess I expected someone to still be there. But why? Why would anyone be willing to stay behind with nothing but monsters roaming the streets? And hey, really, if I had been them, I would have been out of here as well.

I first searched the terminal for any food or water. Then, as another night was coming upon us, I started to barricade the tunnel entrance, hoping it would be enough to secure my location. I then went out onto the tarmac, keeping a close watch for any movement till we arrived at the door leading to the control tower. This door was usually secured, but the code was also common knowledge among pilots, enabling them to access updated weather information. Once the tower door opened, I drew out my Desert Eagle, pointing it directly in front of me ready to fire at first sign of movement. I entered the stairwell leading up to the control tower and slowly climbed the stairs, hugging the walls on either side and switching from one wall to the other to be sure I got a full view of our surroundings. When we reached the top of the stairs, I took a long look around, confirming the emptiness of the structure. George and I now had an excellent view of the surrounding area or at least that part of the island and would be able to see anyone approach us. I just hoped zombies couldn't swim or walk underwater.

We decided to spend the night in the tower but first turned on its beacon, which I hoped would attract the right sort of attention. After watching the dark skies and looking out into the blackness over the lake, I decided to get some shut eye. For the first time since seeing the video and coming to the empty town and city, I felt safe and secure. I raised the antenna of both radios and turned them on. As I settled in one of the controller's chairs, I could feel the tension I had been feeling for a week slowly melt away, and soon, a much-needed deep sleep took me.

CHAPTER 10

I guess I had a good six hours sleep and was jolted awake by some sounds on the CB radio. The fully charged new batteries I had installed back when I had returned to my downed plane had increased its reception. It was chatter; someone was using the radio. As I first awoke, I was disoriented. But slowly the fog of sleep dissipated, and I could now clearly make out the voice on the radio and that she was transmitting a distress call. My first instinct was to lift the mike and respond, but then I stopped myself. Did I really want anyone to know I was alive or my location? I continued to listen to what appeared to be the voice of a young female pleading for help, but no one else replied. She claimed to be a member of a six-person group, four adults and two children, stranded in their apartment and running low on food and water.

I listened to her distress call being repeated every few minutes for some five or so minutes and then turned to George, asking him, "What do you think?"

He just cocked his head and looked at me.

I picked up the radio's mike and then transmitted, "Mayday caller, Mayday caller, what is your twenty? Over." (a twenty or, more so, a ten-twenty in CB lingo means location).

I waited about forty-five seconds and, having got no reply, transmitted again. "Mayday caller, Mayday caller, please identify your twenty? Over."

This time I got a reply. "We are trapped on the sixth floor of our building. Over." This didn't really tell me much.

"Mayday caller, trapped how? Over."

"There are zombies on the lower floors, and we can't get out. We're running low on food and water. Over."

I pictured in my head the runner I had seen as the zombies tore him apart. I had tried to help him, but he had simply been too far away. Now I was going to have to decide if I should help these people. George and I were relatively safe here at the airport tower, and even if we did get overrun, I could commandeer another plane and fly back home to safety. Or was home still safe? Was I even up to fighting numerous zombies to try to rescue people I didn't even know?

Again, I transmitted. "What is your twenty? Where in the city are you? Over."

"Can you come to help us? Over."

"I need to know where you are first. Over."

"We are just off Old Weston Road south of Eglinton. Can you help us please?" she pleaded over the radio.

It was going to be several kilometers travel and through a densely— or what had been densely— populated area, so I suspected it would be full of zombies. Daylight was now breaking, and I knew or thought I knew, this would be the time of fewest zombies on the street. "What do you think, George? Should we go on a rescue mission?"

"What exactly are you requiring? Over," I transmitted over the CB.

"Food and water for my parents, two brothers, and sister. Over"

"Why hadn't you evacuated with the rest of the city? Over."

"My parents speak poor English and didn't understand the orders. So we got left behind, I guess."

"Are you prepared to evacuate now? Over."

"My little brother and sister are very afraid of the zombies; they are only eight and five years old. Over."

Great. Now if I don't help them, I was condemning small children to die. And if I did help them, well, the food would only give them a few extra days, and the children would definitely slow us down as we tried to leave the city.

"George, I wish you could speak so we could talk this out between us."

George gave a couple of sharp barks and began to wag his tail.

"I guess that is your answer. It's going to be a dangerous go, you know; we have to avoid these zombies and then convince the family to come with us to …" To where I had no idea. "Well, we'll decide that when the time comes, maybe back here, as it seems very defensible."

I picked up the mike again and transmitted that we are on our way to them, but it would take several hours unless I could find some sort of transportation. I told them I could bring food and water, but they would have to decide to leave their apartment, or we would leave them on their own. Sounded cruel, but what option did we have?

I found some field glasses the controllers used to spy incoming planes and used them to scan the shoreline. As I expected, there were no zombies in sight. Maybe they didn't like the water like they seemed to not like light. This observation, I hoped, would come in handy, as George and I prepared to leave the tower and the presumed safety of the island. We made a small pathway through our barricade in the tunnel and cautiously covered it up, watching and listening for any sounds or shadows.

Once we were clear of the tunnel, we found our canoe exactly where we left it. I unpacked a shotgun and another high-powered rifle, loaded them with ammunition, and then took several extra boxes to be sure. I still carried my two handguns around my waist. We loaded up a backpack with rations of food and water that should last several days

51

and then covered the canoe again. So far, we had been lucky—no sign of zombies. So we now began our trek to central Etobicoke where this family was trapped.

We began our journey going up Bathurst Street. The main idea was to follow that to St Clair and then St Clair to Old Weston Road. It seemed like a pretty straight route. But as we approached King Street, George went down on his haunches and began a low growl. "Danger ahead?" I softly asked George.

We changed direction and headed west down one of the side streets a couple of blocks and then north again. We waited beside a building as we again approached King Street. Seeing nothing for a few minutes, we then ran as fast as we could to the other side and continued north on this side street. We followed the same procedure crossing Queen Street, but though we had only been traveling an hour the weight of the guns and backpack were starting to exhaust me. And yet, we still had a long way to go. Actually, it wasn't the backpack that bothered me. It was the extra rifle. I was used to carrying one but not three, though I loathed to leave one behind, as I really wouldn't have much time to reload.

Once at Dundas, there was a school / day care, an ideal building to hide behind but also a large playground out in the open that we would have to cross. I communicated with George through some hand gestures that he was to run over to the structure on the playground and hide (lie down), which he did. I then went to join him using a crouch run.

Once we were both there, George again began to growl, and I spotted them—five zombies coming around the corner of the building. I had no time to hide. I just drew a bead on the first one; took off the safety; and fired, getting him between the eyes. I had to drop the other guns from my shoulders as I chambered the next round. It seemed the zombies were moving rapidly, toward me as I dropped two more in rapid succession. George ran at them and tackled one (the Argos would have been impressed) as the bolt of my rifle jammed. I quickly dropped that rifle and pulled out the Desert Eagle, firing at the two remaining zombies' heads. In my rush, I must have fired four rounds but got both. Then I kicked myself for having used up the extra two precious rounds.

I recovered the dropped rifles, unjamming the bolt and chambering another round and then watched to see if more zombies were coming from the sound of the gunshots.

The way seemed clear for now, so we hastily retreated across the street. We crisscrossed several smaller streets as we made our way northwest, but it was getting onto noon, and the warm spring sun was shining. We finally reached Bloor Street, which was deserted of cars but did have a few car dealerships on it. "What do you think, George? Should we see if we can get any keys? Driving will get us there faster."

I broke into the office of one dealership and rummaged through several desks till I came up with some keys. I figured if we were going to commandeer a vehicle, it should be able to take all of us. So I looked for a minivan. The dealership didn't have any, but they did have a cargo van. Other than the front seats, there were none, but people could sit on the floor. I found the key for it just as a small number of zombies came on the scene. Instead of standing and fighting, George and I jumped into the van and tried to start it. It took several jugs and with a backfire and black smoke started up finally—just as the zombies began to swarm us. One tried to grab me through the driver side window, which was, thankfully, closed but I took a bead on him through the closed window and fired the Desert Eagle again, blowing his face away. Then I put the van in gear and began to drive away.

Now I hit Dufferin and proceeded north, crossing the intersection at Dupont and hitting a few zombies along the way. Note to self—they also can't stop speeding vehicles. *Just must hope not to hit a real person. A real person? What am I talking about? These were real people at one time.*

Anyway, there were no other problems till we got to St Clair and headed west again to Old Weston Road. As we got nearer to the family's apartment building, we contacted them on the CB. It was approaching one o'clock in the afternoon when we arrived at the apartment building. We told them to come down and we could get them out of the city; we had a vehicle.

"Someone is banging on our door," the girl replied. "I can only guess it's zombies." As she goes into a panic.

"Are there any others still in the building? Over."

"We aren't sure. We have heard screaming over several nights, and the children are very frightened. Over. They are banging on the door trying to get in. Hurry! Help us please."

"All right. It's going to take some time for us to get upstairs to you. Can you send a rope or something down the side of the building? We can send up a gun or two with ammunition, so your dad and brother can hold them off till I get there? Over."

"Please just hurry!"

"OK. Let me talk to your dad for a minute. Over."

We watched what appeared to be the lobby from a hundred meters out, and I saw several zombies milling around inside the doors. It was a few minutes till I heard a male voice over the radio I guessed was the father. I told him about the conditions in the lobby and asked if he could lower some rope, explaining we would send up some guns and ammo, as well as a little food and 2 bottles of water, just enough to hold them till George and I were able to fight our way up to them. It was hard talking to him, as he reverted to speaking Syrian, his mother tongue, under the duress of the situation.

I finally got him to understand that he should lower something we could tie the backpack and guns to. We could hear the children screaming as he lowered several sheets and blankets tied together. As we pulled the van up to the doors, some of the zombies saw us and began coming toward us. I jumped out, leaving the engine running and quickly tied the backpack and shotgun to the sheets and then radioed for them to start hauling it up.

A couple of zombies had now exited the lobby and were coming at me when George again blindsided them from behind, knocking them off their feet and giving me the precious seconds I needed to draw the Browning and shoot them. I went around to the building's fire escape, which I hoped would be unlocked. The door was ajar, so I slowly opened it and looked inside. The main floor seemed clear here, but I could hear feet shuffling above. I figured this was still going to be my fastest and safest route. So George and I began to climb the steps to the sixth floor. George went into his crouch several times as we ascended the stairs, with me pointing the Browning dead ahead of me, hugging the walls.

In the third-floor stairwell was where we ran into three more zombies, but I had killed two of them even before they knew we were there. I was getting better at these headshots. The third went down after a moment with a look on his face that seemed to ask, *Where did those shots come from?*

We climbed over the zombie bodies and finally got to the sixth floor. We opened the door slightly to look down the hallway and saw seven more zombies trying to gain entry to an apartment and heard the children screaming as they banged at the door. I had to count in my head how many shots I had fired with both the Desert Eagle and the Browning. I turned the volume of the radio way down and told the dad to start firing the shotgun through the door at about head height once he heard my gunfire and to keep firing till the gun was empty. I figured the Desert Eagle only had one left in the chamber and the Browning, maybe six rounds in the mag and chamber. So I changed the magazines in each gun, quietly.

Then, with one gun in each hand, I swung open the door to the fire stairs and began blasting away, dropping three zombies before they were alerted, I was there but firing in such a rapid fashion I knew I'd wasted some rounds. A moment after I came through the door, the dad fired off the shotgun through his door, killing the zombie that had been banging on it. With the next four rounds, he also killed another one as I was making my way to his door, dropping every zombie in sight. This battle only lasted less than a minute. But in the end, seven more zombies had been eliminated. How many more to go would be anyone's guess.

CHAPTER 11

I went over the count again—seven destroyed zombies, five by me and the two in front of their door. However, I had used up nineteen rounds of ammo plus the five shotgun shells. We just could not sustain this wastage of precious ammo. We would need to do much better. As I approached their door, I yelled out that I was outside and the way was now clear. I heard their door lock slide open, and timidly and slowly, they opened the door. I hurried to get inside and gave them instructions so we could leave quickly. I told them to pack a bag for each with a few changes of clothes. They just stood there, hesitating. I looked at them and said, "Don't you understand? I have to get you all out of here and to a safe place."

At this, the father began to speak rapidly. I had trouble understanding him. But the girl, a teen, began to interpret what her dad was saying.

They had come from Syria as refugees, having lived in a refugee camp for several years. In fact, their youngest was born in a refugee camp, and they wouldn't go into that type of living again. I wasn't sure what to say. I did know the experience many had in refugee camps, and it wasn't nice. I couldn't offer them a guarantee that they wouldn't be again placed in such a place. But then I told them of my hunt camp and that I had several now vacant cabins; they could stay there if they wished.

The mother and father looked at each other and finally agreed to this. While we had been talking, George had suddenly gotten to his feet and given a small growl. Damn. Some zombies had already returned, I thought. But then we heard someone calling out in the hall.

Startled, the older brother said, "That's Joshua, one of our neighbors."

This information caught me completely off guard. "There are others still on this floor?" I asked.

They just shrugged, and we quickly let a young man in his mid-twenties into the apartment. Once inside and seeing the family readying to leave, he stated that his wife and two children were still in his apartment, where they had been hiding till they'd heard the gunfire. They too wanted help to safety. Both his children were toddlers, only four and two years old. This was going to really slow us down. I told him and the older brother to go through the hallway and see if there were any more people still on this floor. I let them take the other rifle, which was the .22 and told the young father to have his wife pack a couple of bags of clothing for themselves and the kids. Then I rechecked my ammo situation. I was now down to only one magazine for each handgun. So, I reloaded both but decided I would only use the Browning. I had to find some more ammo, though, or both guns would be useless before long.

It took fifteen more minutes for everyone to be ready. The younger children wanted to take their toys with them, but we had little room. To compromise and to stop the crying, I agreed to one toy each. There apparently were no others on the floor. So now we were responsible for getting ten strangers out of a building crawling with zombies.

George and I took the lead Rashad, the oldest son in the Syrian family, who I guessed to be in his late teens, carrying the .22 in the middle and his father, John, a tall, capable-looking man, bringing up the rear, shotgun at the ready. We got to the fire stairs without a problem and then proceeded down, telling the children to be as quiet as mice.

We were about to get down to the second floor when we were confronted by several zombies. I shot the nearest two, and we backed away. The father wanted us to retreat to the roof. But I was firm. "We would be trapped on the roof," I told him. "And if the zombies didn't get us, hunger and thirst would. We have to fight our way through. It's our only chance.

So, with George in the lead, we three with guns came around the corner of the stairway and fired into the zombies. It only took maybe ten to fifteen seconds, but the echo of the gunfire now had the youngest children crying. I used only four more rounds, but that still gave me only six left in the Browning.

Both riflemen emptied their guns as I rushed the mothers and kids down the remaining stairs to the first floor. I made them reload their guns while I checked the door. The van was still running, but it was some fifty meters from the door. The little ones simply wouldn't be able to make that run. I told them I would go out and get the van and bring it to the door, and the older brother said he would come with me to open the side door. We gave his .22 to the other father as we got ready to run to the van.

The door to the main floor began to open, and we had to jam it closed to prevent the zombies from entering. Then we bolted through the side door, making a mad dash for the van. Once inside, I put the van in gear and crossed the lawn while the boy slid open the side door. I blew the horn, and everyone came rushing out. The toddlers were loaded into the van first, followed by the women. Finally, the fathers climbed in, sliding the door closed as I spun the tires on the grass to make our getaway. We bounced off the curb, and everyone went flying all over the place as we escaped. Some of the kids (and adults) got bumped up, not having any seatbelts on. Only where to go?

The gas tank light was now a solid red. Vehicles on car lots would have just enough gas for an estimated test drive to discourage theft. We had succeeded in getting away from the apartment only to be running out of gas. Things weren't looking good. We passed a hardware store, so I stopped there to get some garden hose. Some of the people wondered what I was doing, but the older father immediately knew where I was going with this.

We found several cars deserted in a parking lot, and with the two younger men and George standing watch, we siphoned gas out of those vehicles and filled our van. I just wasn't sure it would be enough to get me back home. But it would get us to the airport, so I decided that was where we should go first. It was defendable and had food and water to last likely a good bit of a month. Plus, I could always fly us out if need be. I had seen a Cessna 401 parked at the airport; I had often rented that type of plane to pick up customers from the United States.

On our way back down to Billy Bishop Airport, I swung around to my wrecked aircraft to retrieve the supplies I had put in there, as I knew I wouldn't be able to fly all ten people out in it. Now, with several more guns and a few thousand rounds of ammunition, I no longer worried about my handguns. And with four or five of us to do the shooting, I figured our odds of surviving had increased dramatically.

We then proceeded down the highway to the Gardner Expressway and across till we reached a turnoff for the airport. Dusk was coming, and we were seeing more zombies taking to the streets. So once at the airport tunnel, we went in carrying what we could and locking the rest in the van. We should be able to get it in the morning. I guided everyone through the small route I had left in the blockade using glow sticks to light the path.

Once in the terminal, we began by feeding the children while the men set up more blockades from the tunnel as fallback positions. Once everyone had eaten, I led them all up to the tower, where we could spy everything along the channel shoreline, as well as the lake. I put on the beacon again, though I wasn't sure why. We agreed to take turns keeping watch while we put the children to bed on the floor of the control tower. I also turned on the radio sets for the tower in the unlikely chance we'd catch a transmission. But then again, less than twenty-four hours ago, I had not heard their distress call.

I looked over these ten strangers as I took my turn at the watch from midnight to 2:00 a.m. and watched out of the control tower for any signs of zombies. The world seemed so peaceful now and worth saving—or at least this small part of it did. Watching the children sleep brought back memories of watching over my own kids while they slept. It again made me wonder what had happened to them. Were they alive? Or had they somehow become zombies?

Then a thought jumped into my mind. If I came across my son or daughter and they had become a zombie, would I be able to shoot them?

But back to the here and now—I watched from the safety of the tower as hundreds, maybe thousands of zombies took to the streets again. But they never came anywhere near the lake. Were they for some reason afraid of or avoiding the water? I of course did not have the answer, just the questions, but it gave me something to think about. At 2:00 a.m., I awoke Joshua, the young father, to take his turn watching, and then George and I went off to slumber land ourselves.

CHAPTER 12

At about 6:00 a.m., I felt a weight that seemed to be crushing my chest and thought that George was laying over me, so I sleepily told him to get off. Then giving me a shock, he pushed his wet nose into my hand. I startled awake, only to find the baby girl lying on my chest sleeping. Though it was a start, I tried not to move or wake her but just patted the top of her head, and George pushed his wet nose in under my other hand so I had to pat his head as well. I smiled and whispered, "You jealous?"

Gingerly, I took the girl off my chest and lay her off to one side.

Her mother was awake and watched me put her child off to my side and smiled. In a low voice, she told me that her daughter must like me to be willing to cuddle up so. Great. Now I would feel totally miserable if I could not get their family to safety. But I still didn't know how or where that would be.

We had done a reasonable job securing this site, putting up several blockades through the tunnel, and had decided we could just keep watch from the tower, as we would be able to monitor the entrance to the tunnel from there. We set up one person there with a radio. Then the rest of us would stay in the terminal. And we were also able to let the children out onto the tarmac to run and play midday. That didn't seem to draw any attention from the zombies for the first day or two.

Each night, I would continue to turn on the beacon should anyone see it. Plus, we kept a person in the tower to listen to the radios. We used camp stoves to cook some meals. The kids resisted the dehydrated foods at first but eventually developed a taste for the meals, as it was all we had. We still slept up in the tower, mainly because it was our last place of defense if the other defenses were breached, and we wouldn't have time to move the children while trying to fight the zombies. Every couple of hours, we would transmit a Mayday over the UHF radios from the tower. But with no reply, it was beginning to seem a waste of time.

Then hell began to break out on our fourth night on the island. As our observer watched, some of the zombies began to go to the entrance of the tunnel. What had caused them to finally start to try and get across to us, we have no real idea. But try they did. Some went into the tunnel entrance, while others walked out to the water's edge. But after a couple fell off the pier and didn't seem to surface, we figured they couldn't swim.

The women took the children back up to the tower, while the rest of us manned the first barricade. The women then got some of the rifles to start shooting the zombies before they entered the tunnel. We set a fire in the first barricade, hoping the flames would stop them. And it did for a while. The few that tried to go through the flames were shot by us at the second barricade. The women also engaged some of the zombies as they stood at the edge of the pier. In total, I would guess we killed near a hundred zombies before they seemed to retreat and regroup—if that were possible. This battle only lasted fifteen minutes before the zombies stopped. But now we had to keep two people down in the tunnel ready for the next attack. This would wear our nerves thin. Again, we sent out a Mayday over the UHF radio, though we decided to not use the beacon that night—just in case that was what was attracting the zombies.

All was quiet for a couple of hours. Then a second wave seemed to attack. Because they moved slowly, we had good advance warning they were coming. We watched them assemble on the streets north of the airport, and they formed a bottleneck as they tried to enter the tunnel. With the high-powered rifles, the women again began picking them off as they slumbered down the street but this time there must have been a thousand of them. They were able to get maybe as many as fifty of them while we manned the tunnel barricades.

By now, the fire we had set in the first attack had died, having exhausted its fuel, and left nothing but ash and charred furniture. We spread some avgas on the remains in the hopes there would still be enough flame to keep the zombies out and ignited the barricade for a second time just as three zombies made their way pass the barricade. They tried to grab Joshua, who set the fire, but I shot two with my Desert Eagle and John (the father from Syria) blew away the third with a blast from the 12-gauge shotgun. Through the flames, we fired volley after volley of ammunition, dropping zombies in the dozens. But still they kept coming till there was literally no space left in the tunnel entrance. It was piled high with bodies. The stench of dead flesh was what required us to withdraw to our third barrier.

At the third barrier, we had fresh guns and lots of extra ammunition, and we were able to get some rest while the women watched the movements of the zombies from the safety of the control tower. There were still several hundred zombies waiting to try to get to us. But for now, they were stopped again.

A third wave then attacked an hour or so later. The zombies were literally crawling over their fallen companions which did slow them down but did not stop them, they just kept coming.

We had set up two skirmish lines of defense with two of us (John and me) at the second barricade and the other two men at the third and final tunnel barricade. The first barricade had now been reduced to ashes, so the zombies just crawled over their fallen comrades and were then free to attack our second barricade. We fought them as much as possible, emptying magazine after magazine of ammunition into the crowds. But still they kept on coming. Soon, the four of us had fired so many rounds that our rifle barrels were turning red-hot. So we would have to drop that gun and go onto the next one. But they kept coming.

The zombies finally made it to our second barricade and, by sheer numbers, overwhelmed us. John and I had to retreat to the third barricade as the zombies broke through the defenses. John tried to shoot a couple more in our retreat but stumbled. The zombies were on him before any of us had a chance to react.

We had also set up some cocktails of avgas, and as the zombies overran the second barricade, we lit them and threw them at the attacking horde. This was finally enough to end their third wave attack but at a very heavy price for us. We were all quiet as we watched more flames claim more of the zombies. Rashad, John's son, broke down and cried as we held him back from climbing over this last barricade to his dead father's side.

CHAPTER 13

I t was now approaching the morning of our fifth day at the island airport. We hadn't yet told the women of our loss as we yet prepared for another onslaught of zombies. Hundreds of spent casings littered the floor of the tunnel, as well as what appeared to be some two hundred or more zombie bodies. The stench of the decaying and burning bodies was overwhelming. And on several occasions, we had to excuse ourselves to go and wretch. None of us in the tunnel thought any less of the others for this.

Upon a closer inspection, it was discovered, to our amazement, that we were running low on ammunition. The thousands of rounds I had successfully commandeered from the Sails store were meant to last us a long time. But the reality was we'd had to use up so much in the first night of battle that our supply could very soon end. What we, I, had failed to consider was the sheer volume of zombies that would be able to attack. Ideally, we would have had great advantage by them being jammed into a bottleneck coming through the tunnel, giving us plenty of time to properly aim and shoot them as they advanced. However, they had launched so many of themselves at us—and had no fear of the consequence of death since they were already dead—that we had been forced to fire rapidly into their advancing lines without the time to take careful aim, wasting hundreds of bullets. We were going to need some other way to block the tunnel.

Fire and barricades alone weren't going to do it. We needed to collapse the tunnel in some way. The tunnel itself was made of likely brick and mortar. But how thick would its walls be? It ran under the water of the channel into the Port of Toronto. So reasonably, if we could blow a hole in it the channel, water would be able to flood the tunnel, thus closing off that means of attack. It would also close off that means of escape for us or for much needed resupplies. We also needed to know where to find enough explosives to blow the hole in the wall but not get ourselves blown to bits in the process. After the long night's battle, we were too tired to give this much more thought.

Suddenly, we heard shots coming from the tower with the women and children.

We immediately took our positions behind the third and last barricade, figuring the zombies were mounting yet another attack from shore. But then we heard on the radio from the women that some zombies were approaching from the east. At first, this appeared confusing, as the main entrance of the airport was by the tunnel leading to the north. So how were the zombies able to approach from the east if they couldn't swim? However, the island airport was situated on only one of several islands all interconnected with bridges in the Port of Toronto with three main islands—Ward's Island to the east; Center Island basically in the middle; and Hanlon's Point, where the airport was located. Center Island was a big tourist draw, and Ward's Island was home to a small, artistic community village. This, I figured, was where these zombies were coming from, as the only other way onto the islands was by ferry, and I didn't really think the zombies could control a ferry.

Rashad had remained in the tunnel on our side, while Joshua and I ran to the tower. As we got to the top of the tower's stairs, I was handed the night-vison binoculars. And with the sun just beginning to rise, I looked in the direction Saleem, John's older daughter, indicated. About a hundred meters from the tower to the east was a three-meter-high chain-link fence to keep people safely away from the runways. And on the other side of the fence were several zombies. The fence covered the whole eastern part of the airport lands except for a single gate for vehicular traffic. I figured the zombies had not shown any sort of dexterity in fence climbing, so we could be reasonably safe, apart from the gate or any holes in the fence. We would need to take a closer look. In the meantime, Joshua and I took our time in shooting the few zombies by the fence just to be on the safe side.

Now we briefed the women on the results of the three waves of attacks on the tunnel that night, explaining that it seemed our best chance on the island was to render the tunnel unusable but that, to do so, would also mean closing off one possible escape route or means of resupply.

Then after some discussion came the time I had been trying to avoid and dreaded—telling John's wife and family she was now a widow and that he had fallen in that night's battle. As the sounds of wailing began to take form, Joshua went to the tunnel to relieve Rashad and told him his family now knew of their father's fate. I had broken the news and now went on to glumly start to prepare the breakfast.

After breakfast, Joshua, Rashad, and I got some sleep while the women took over the watch. George and Joey, John's younger boy, were tasked with looking after the younger children playing catch frisbee while we slept and, later, discussed our next moves.

Saleem was taking her turn down in the tunnel, going over in her mind what had been said at breakfast about having to find a way to block or flood the tunnel, keeping her mind occupied with anything but the body of her dead father, which lay only a few meters away. She climbed over the last barrier with a lantern to take a closer look at the walls. Holding the lantern a few inches away, she made a closer inspection of the tiles covering the walls down to the base where the tiles touched the floor. She continued her inspection till she came to what had been the second barrier and had to stop due to the piled carnage that blocked the way. She began to develop an idea.

CHAPTER 14

The men were awoken around noon on this fifth day on the islands. We'd had no more contact with the zombies we expected had come from Ward's Island that day. But possible zombies on the connected islands, was now a concern to us as we discussed our current situation, which was frankly looking grimmer, over lunch. The women were encouraged to participate in the discussions, as they did as much of the fighting as the men. But Marcia, John's widow, was very much old-school Muslim and would not voice her opinion in public.

This was when Saleem presented her ideas. With a map we'd found of the Toronto Islands, including the tunnel, we pointed out several locations in our favor, as well as several possible dangers. We knew our weakest point at this time was the tunnel, and we likely wouldn't be able to hold off another attack like that of the previous night. We agreed the simplest solution was to cave in the tunnel or otherwise flood it, but we again faced the problem of how to blow up the tunnel. Saleem pointed out that only a kilometer away was both York naval reserve post and Fort York Armories, suggesting we could find some form of explosive in either site. This would mean we would need the tunnel intact at least for the time being, as it was our access to the mainland. It was also point out that we would need the tunnel to get fresh supplies of food and water, not to mention ammunition, so the easiest solution may not be the right solution. But how then to block the tunnel from another attack tonight or tomorrow?

Saleem suggested we block off the entrance to the tunnel at the Tip Top Tailor building instead using material from that side of the tunnel. There were still plenty of warehouses in the immediate area that we could use crates from. But if we were going to do it, we needed to start right away to get it done before dusk. It was a little past 1:30, so we had maybe three to four hours to find items and block the entrance to the tunnel.

We scanned the area with the binoculars and only saw a few small bands of zombies walking the streets. Loading up with a couple of rifles and a hundred rounds of ammo for each of us, we ventured down to the tunnel and slowly proceeded through, climbing over the dead till we reached the other side at Tip Top's. To say it was icky going through those bodies would be an understatement.

On the other side, we watched for several minutes to see if any zombies had detected our presence. It was Joshua, Rashad, Saleem, and me while the two mothers stayed with their children. As there was no indication the zombies were aware of us, we continued to the next building, which was a residence and would not be helpful. Staying low, we ran across the road and there found a warehouse. Once inside, we needed to break a window to gain entry. We looked around till we found some shipping doors. We also split up, looking for some kind of forklift to move the heavy crates into position but didn't find any. What we did find was some handheld trucks, which were used to move the crates around. As this was the best we could find, we had to use them. Bringing the first crate out onto the loading dock, we found there was no way to get it to the ground. We then had to go back into building and find another exit. Finding that, we broke through another door and were about to drag the crates across the street when some zombies came around a corner.

Dropping our loads, we quickly unslung our rifles and began to fire into the pack of zombies. We must have taken them by surprise as they just stood there, like they were startled. After we had eliminated them, I instructed Rashad and Saleem to leave their trucks alone and, instead, keep watch for more zombies. Saleem originally objected, but I told her we would come back for their loads as time permitted and again began to pull my crated truck into the Tip Top building. With Saleem and Rashid keeping watch for us, Joshua and I continued bring more crates into the Tip Top building and blocking most of the entrance. There were a couple more zombies making their way toward us, but Saleem and Rashad made quick order in killing them.

Finally, with twelve crates to block the way, we began to organize them so the zombies could not get in but we would still be able to get out, leaving one of the trucks nearby so we could move things if and as needed. One of the obstacles we set up was blocking the door entry to the building, while a second was blocking the tunnel entrance for the most part.

We used what daylight we had left to spilt into three groups—one to recheck our perimeter, specifically the fence on the eastern side of the airport; the mothers to bathe and feed the youngest of the children; and the last group, Joey and me, to ensure our escape route. Saleem, Rashad, and Joshua made up the first group. Together, the three followed along the fence line to check for any holes or gaps that the zombies might be able to use to breach that defensive. The gateway for vehicular traffic was the only thing found, and though it did appear securely locked, they decided to drive one of the maintenance vehicles up against it to give it some added strength. This now done, they went back to the tower to eat and, in turns, sponge bathe.

Meanwhile, I went searching for the keys to be able to enter the twin-engine Cessna 401, which I did eventually find in the office of one of the charter companies. As I said, my little group was Joey, George, and me. So I designated Joey to be my copilot, which seemed to perk up his spirits after having lost his dad the night before. With the keys in hand, I then began a circle check of the plane, checking on the wing gas tanks and the engine compartments, as well as the oil and the propellers to see there were no dents or cracks. That done, I then went on to check the fuselage body and then unlocked the door to the main cabin. Opening it allowed the steps to drop down, so we went up them into the cabin, me with drawing my Browning just in case any zombies were somehow on board.

The plane was obviously for some executive, as it had seating for eight passengers, as well as a bar, fridge, and microwave oven. I could see Joey's dark eyes as they grew wide, finally seeing how the top 10 percent of society lived and traveled. We then proceeded to the plane's cockpit and sat down in the pilots' seats.

My mission at this point was to ensure we had a means of escape from the island should the need arise, and this seemed our best option—if it was flyable, that is. The plane had been sitting on the tarmac for at least two weeks or longer. So I figured the batteries would be low and needed to be recharged, which I would do during a preflight check and maybe just run the engines for about fifteen minutes to do the charging. I pointed out the gauges I wanted Joey to watch for me while I did a full systems check. It was mostly the RPM gauges, and I told him to let me know if and when the RPMs dropped below 1,000; it would happen several times while I tested the throttle and fuel mixtures, but it gave him a much-needed feeling of importance to be a crew member. I also explained the startup procedure to him, telling him that the engines would be counted as engine number one on the starboard (left) side and number two on the port (right) side.

Then having turned on the electrical system, I looked out the starboard side window and declared, "Clear one." At this, Joey slid forward on his seat to see my side of the plane and confirmed the number one engine was clear of people or obstacles. "Turning one," I declared.

And I started the ignition of the number one engine. It sputtered a few times but finally started with some backfiring, not too good a sign. But I got it calmed down and running at a 1000 RPMs smoothly.

I then looked out the port window and said, "Clear two."

At this, Joey looked out his window and said, "Clear two."

"Turning two," I said as I tried to start the number two engine. But it sputtered and died a couple of times before finally starting. I had to manipulate the throttle and mixture several times to get it running at a steady 1000 RPMs. Due to the drain on the batteries, I decided to just let the engines run for the first five minutes at the 1000 RPMs to recharge before proceeding with the rest of a preflight checklist.

As both engines were now functioning smoothly and the checklist was complete, I let the engines continue to run for several more minutes as I checked on the other flight controls, namely the ailerons, elevators, and rudder. The fuel tanks were showing half full, so I really wanted to fill them. With no electricity to run the pumps, however, the only way would be to use jerry cans of avgas, but this could be extremely dangerous in and of itself. If there was a single spark from the static electricity produced from the fuel going into the tanks, it would not only explode the fuel in the jerry can but also the fuel already in the wing tanks and the plane as a whole. That was why airlines usually made passengers disembark while refueling.

After completing the checks on all the systems and satisfied as to their working order, I ran the engines for an extra fifteen minutes just to be sure. Joey and I then searched for some jerry cans to load fuel into. But as dusk was setting in, I decided not to siphon any fuel from the other aircraft today.

We enjoyed a dinner of fresh chicken and vegetable stew that we had found while searching the warehouse earlier that day. Having fresh rather than dehydrated foods increased our cravings for more fresh food, so we began to plan on returning to the mainland in the morning to see what more we could find. It would also be a time for us to inspect the two armories nearby as suggested by Saleem.

As dusk descended, we kept a careful watch on the entrance to the tunnel on the mainland side to see if the zombies would be able to breach the new barricades we had set up. It was with relief that we saw that, despite their numbers, they were unable to get past those barricades. Though we would have been able to shoot many zombies as they got stopped at the Tip Top Tailors building, we instead stood down for the night and used the night to get more much-needed rest and save our rapidly diminishing ammo. We also had to pay more attention to our eastern fence, but though a handful of zombies did seem to show up at the fence, they were unable to get past it. We also decided that, once we got back in the morning to our expedition to the mainland, we would also go to the other islands to hunt down and clear them of any zombies.

That night as we watched the zombies from across our side of the channel, safely in the control tower, we were able to count somewhere between three hundred and five hundred zombies as they tried to gain entrance to the tunnel. In silence, Joshua, Rashad, and I just kept glancing between each of us and the pack of zombies across the water and silently understood we would not have been able to stop so many. With the entrance blocked to them, they didn't seem too organized in passing it so just wandered around till the morning, when they dispersed.

CHAPTER 15

We used only one person per shift for a lookout that night as we were confident the zombies wouldn't breach the barricade. At 6:30 in the morning, we were all up having breakfast, and we discussed our plans to check the two armories. We had originally figured just the three men would go. But Saleem objected to this. She wanted very much to be part of the force to do in the zombies, and she repeatedly reminded us that the two armories had been her idea in the first place.

After some fifteen minutes, we relented and agreed to her coming with us and decided we would then break up into pairs, each going to their respective armory. This plan's inherent risk was that there were fewer to fight any possible zombies. But we figured it was worth the threat, as we would be able to investigate both sites at the same time, thus cutting our exposure in half. Also, since the sites were so close to one another, if one team ran into trouble, the second team would be close enough to assist. We decided we would go an hour after sunrise, about 8:00 a.m.

As we loaded up our rifles and took about sixty extra rounds of ammunition, Joshua said we wouldn't have had enough ammunition to have stopped them last night if they had breached the barricade. Saleem and Rashad just froze for a moment.

"That's why we need to get more guns and ammo from the armories," I said. "It will mean the difference of survival for us if we fail."

The group was silent as we all thought about this.

It was about ten minutes to eight as we walked down the tower stairs, crossed the tarmac to the terminal building, and made our way to our side of the tunnel. We had to climb through the barricade we still had up at our point in the tunnel. George followed us till I stopped him in the tunnel and told him he was to, "Protect the children by not letting any of the zombies get through the tunnel." Then we proceeded up the other end of the tunnel. We still had CB radios, so we used those to contact the women still watching out the tower to see that the way was clear.

With all clear, we used the fork truck to move aside some of the crates we had set up first at the tunnel entrance and then again at the entrance of to the Tip Top Tailor building. We tried to make the opening just wide enough to squeeze through, but this would be a death trap for us if we had to retreat in a hurry. We just hoped that wouldn't happen. The van we had used in our escape from the apartment building a few days earlier was still sitting there with the keys in the ignition. So we decided why walk if we could ride. The engine did cough a bit but wasn't any real problem turning over, so we backed up Bathurst Street to Lakeshore Boulevard. Then we headed west to the Princess Gates at the opening to the CNE grounds and parked there. From here on, we would go on foot to the two armories, which both were within several hundred meters.

Joshua and Rashad then headed off for the York naval armory, while Saleem and I headed to the Fort York armory in the opposite direction, agreeing to meet back at the van in about an hour to an hour and a half. Saleem and I leapfrogged up the roadway leading to Old Fort York and the armory, taking cover wherever we could to keep as out of sight as possible. We had to circle around a few times to avoid some small bands of zombies but otherwise were uninhibited.

Eventually, we made it to the doors of the armory. These were very thick wooden doors a few inches thick and solidly bolted closed. The windows were few and higher up than could be reached, with heavy steel bars blocking them. At first visual inspection the building looked to be totally impenetrable. There was, however, a courtyard often used for drill practice and parades, as well as for storage of vehicles. It was surrounded by a three-meter-high chain-link fence with several army trucks, affectionately known as deuces for being two and a half-ton trucks, as well as several armored vehicles commonly known as armored cars since they were wheeled rather than tracked vehicles. (During Canada's FLQ crisis in the 1970s, then Prime Minister P. Trudeau had order the army to help in the situation. But the tank tracks had made such a mess of the streets of Montreal that Canada had gone to using wheeled vehicles instead.) I knew the armored cars to be named either Cougars or Grizzlies, depending on their size.

There was a gate over on the eastern side of the parade square, so we made our way to it. As expected, it was fastened with a padlock and chain. We were able to pull the gate open just a few inches but not nearly enough for me to squeeze through. Saleem, on the other hand, with some contorting of her slim, teenaged body, was finally able to slip through the gate. I then passed her the .410-gauge pump-action shotgun through the opening. I knelt and told Saleem to first check the inside area for any zombies and then find something we could use to break the lock and chain for my entry. I kept watch on the outside of the fence while Saleem went about her chores.

After what seemed like forever but was really only ten minutes or so, she came back with a tire iron, which we placed between a link in the chain holding the gate closed, working it to spread apart the link so we could remove it, thus breaking the chain.

Once I, too, was inside the parade square, we inspected the vehicles to see what we could scrounge from them. There was nothing in the trucks, but the armored cars were also locked up with padlocks. We tried several times to pry open the locks with the crowbar but couldn't get it down onto the lock. Finally, I decided we would tempt fate.

I drew my Desert Eagle from its holster, placed the barrel right up against the metal bar of the lock, and fired. This obliterated the lock, and we threw what was left of it to the ground and opened the back door of a Grizzly. We looked inside to find an empty troop carrier. Checking the storage bins, we found them empty as well.

Discouraged but now more determined to find something, we repeated the same thing with the next grizzly. Watching for any sign of movement approaching the armory, we again fired into the lock to the vehicle; only this time, we were rewarded. Inside on the floor was an M60 heavy machine gun, with a three-legged mount. The M60, a belt-fed gun that fired standard 7.62 NATO ammo weapon, had been used since the Vietnam War and was known as the pig for its heavy weight and firepower. With it, we also found four boxes of ammunition, which could be attached to the gun with 480 belt-fed rounds. The only drawback we could see was how the two of us would get such a heavy weapon and ammunition to the van.

Joshua radioed us to check on what was happening. He had heard two gunshots, but as they'd been timed a while between, he assumed we weren't in immediate danger. He also reported that, like us, they had run up against a very well-closed building so hadn't gained entry. This was disappointing but not unexpected. We arranged for him and Rashad to return to the van and then drive it up to the gate at our armory to pick us up—along with our newly acquired M60 with ammo.

While awaiting the arrival of the van, we continued to inspect the third armored car, a Cougar this time. After shooting off its lock, we found one rifle with five loaded magazines and three extra boxes of rounds, which gave us a haul from that vehicle of over a hundred rounds of ammunition to go with the rifle. Two guns and over a thousand rounds of ammunition may sound impressive, but we knew it was only a small drop in the bucket of what we were facing.

Once we loaded up our catch in the van, we returned to reality. We had several more hours to search for more food, but our need for more guns and ammo was imminent. I'd seen a couple of grocery stores when I'd first begun my rescue of this group. Plus, I knew of another army surplus store in the area of Bathurst and Queen Streets. But I had no idea if any of these potential resources still existed. We decided to check them out anyway.

We first went to Queen and Bathurst to check on the army surplus store, which, to my surprise, we found still there. All four of us now together, we entered the store cautiously, watching for any movement. Though it was daylight, the store itself was dark. We found some glow sticks, which we each used to light up some of the store. It was awkward to hold the glow stick and our rifles at the same time. So we would, like in the Sails store, just open them, and place them in the aisles.

We found the racks that used to contain the rifles, but they were all empty, another disappointment. However, when we checked the cabinets, which we'd found locked and had broken open, we discovered boxes of ammunition. We had hit a jackpot. There were drawers full of standard ammunition, including rounds for .22 caliber, 30-odd-6, .303/.308 for our high-powered rifles as well as 12-20- and 410-gauge ammo for our shotguns. I even found four boxes of 9mm rounds for my Browning but nothing for the Desert Eagle.

We grabbed a couple of knapsacks and filled them with the ammunition. Then just as we found the knives and machetes, we were surprised by first one and then a group of zombies in the other parts of the store. For Joshua, it became a problem of having to drop his knapsack and fire his gun into the zombies, as they'd surprised us. This hesitation caused him to be wounded by one of the zombies with several scratches. While fighting off the attack we attempted to bandage his wounds as best we could. We at that time had no idea what those scratches would lead to. After the battle we redressed his bandages and put disinfectant all over the wounds. We then regrouped and headed off to the grocery stores nearby.

We saw from the outside zombies wandering in the first grocery store we came to so just stayed in the van and headed for the next one several blocks away. Seeing no zombies from the outside, we entered the store and began looking for food. It appeared the store had already been looted, as most of the shelves were emptied and the freezers had nothing but bad meat. This second store was then a bust, and we thought we needed to get back to our island.

We did stop at a third grocery store, though, and on checking it out, we found a couple of packages of meat still good at the very bottom of the freezer. We figured the meat on the top had kept the bottom meat cold enough to stay good. But again, as we were leaving, we encountered several zombies. They attacked in what appeared larger numbers, and several of us, having emptied our guns, had to resort to fighting them off with the machetes. It seemed curious that their numbers each time we encountered them would increase. Now we were also finding them starting to be out in the street. So with the guns, ammunition, and the small amount of meat we had scrounged, we made our way back to the Tip Top Tailor building.

As more zombies appeared, we unloaded the van of our bounty. And while Joshua and I fought off the zombies assembling around us, Rashad and Saleem carried the material past the first barricade. Now the mothers across the channel also engaged, firing on the zombies to help give us protecting cover.

As I had expected, it was hell trying to retreat through the small gap we had left in the mainland barricades. Trying to lift the heavy machine gun, as well as the knapsacks of ammunitions, up and over the barricade was taking time—too much time really. As we protected that small gap in the front barricade, Saleem and now Joshua started to take our supplies over the second barricade. Still the zombies seemed to keep on coming, even though they were exposing themselves to daylight.

Joshua set up the M60 at the second barricade to give us cover fire while we closed off the first. The thunderous sounds of the rapid firing of the gun made us hesitate at first. But then we closed off the gap, and with Joshua still manning the M60, we closed the second gap.

Now with both gaps closed, the zombies appeared to stop coming at us, and there was what we hoped would be a long lull in the action. The use of the M60 had destroyed the floor-to-ceiling windows at the front of the building. This now concerned me, as the windows had helped to block the zombies from coming at us totally out numbered.

As we now went through the tunnel and approached the control tower, Joey began to scream and point at the eastern fence; several zombies approached it. We fired a few shots to warn them off. But instead, as always, it seemed they just kept coming. Rashad and I carried the M60 on its tripod up to the tower as Saleem and Joshua brought up the knapsacks of ammo and food. George had joined us from the tunnel and was barking to add to all the commotion.

More zombies were approaching from the mainland side. Even though it was daylight, hundreds of them were coming down Lakeshore Blvd, as well as Bathurst Street. It appeared they were going to launch their strongest offensive yet. We set up the M60, put the extra ammo boxes beside it and started firing. In under a minute, we had fired off the entire box of 480 rounds, dropping numerous zombies along the street. While most of us fired on them from the tower to the mainland, Joshua and I shot the ones at the fence. But it looked like for each one we would kill another took its place. The same thing for the street side; one would fall, and two more would take its place. We figured that, with the power of sheer numbers, they would breach the barricades regardless of our fight. I sent Joey and the women to remove the wheel chocks from the 401 and get the children on board the plane. We hadn't finished refueling, but what we had was going to have to do.

Joshua collapsed during the fight. He seemed to be running a fever, and the wounds he'd suffered earlier at the hands of the zombies were causing him extreme pain. I pulled back some of the bandaging and saw what can only be described as a gross green infection. Our eyes locked on each other for a long moment. I could see tears forming in the young father's eyes. We went to Rashad and Saleem and helped them with the M60 firing on the mainland just meters away.

We were down to the last box of ammo for it when Joshua told us to get to the plane while he held them off. Saleem said no, but I understood what Joshua was preparing to do. He said it was imperative that his wife and children got to safety, and he would hold out if possible. Rashad saw his torn bandages and then saw the awful infection that was spreading through his friend's body. As young as he was, he now understood the sacrifice his friend was about to make and pulled his sister toward the stairs and the tower's exit.

I picked up one of the knapsacks that contained food and grabbed some ammunition from the other and followed the brother and sister. We heard the rat-a-tat-tat from the M60 as we ran across the tarmac to the plane and threw the bags on board. We saw some of the zombies breach the fence, and I yelled for the children to be buckled in. George had attacked a couple of zombies that had breached the tunnel, ripping into their legs, and then joined us as I started the engines.

Joey was ready in the right (copilot) seat and followed my lead, though it wasn't the startup procedures we had practiced. He still told me that the number two engine was clear, and I took off the brakes, and we began to roll down the taxiway to the runway. As we were rolling, we could hear Joshua's wife start to scream that we were leaving Joshua behind as the M60 continued its rat-a-tat-tat. Fighting off the women, Rashad told them Joshua was already dead as he pulled the plane's door closed. Joey and George just looked over at me while I prepared the plane for flight.

A Cessna 401 was said to have a range of about 2,000 kilometers when first out of the factory. Like any machine, however, its maximums decreased over time, and we didn't have full tanks to begin with. So I gave us about 1,200 kilometers of safe range. We took off still hearing the M60 firing as we began to climb into the air. The only question we had to answer now was in what direction to fly.

As the plane rolled down the taxiway, I went over the controls once again that I wanted Joey to report to me and where the switch was to raise the landing gear once we were Airborne, though I would actually be watching the gauges myself. He was to report any changes on the instrument panel, just as a copilot would do while I checked the functions of the controls, the fuel mixture, the brakes, and the throttle, as well as the rudder and ailerons. I proceeded to the eastern end of Runway 27 and only stopped for a moment as I ran up the engines. At 2,700 rpms, Joey stated, "That's 75 percent power."

I held down the brakes as I continued to apply power.

And at 3,000 rpms, Joey stated, "That's 90 percent power."

Still applying even more throttle, I released the brakes and stated, "Rolling," to indicate we were on our takeoff run.

Joey kept a close watch on our indicated speed and reported to me, "V-1," as we met the minimum speed for flight. A few seconds later, he said, "V-2." This was the maximum speed with which to safely abort a takeoff. After his report of V-2, I began to draw back on the control wheel, lifting the plane nose first into the air, having confirmed his report by saying, "Rotate."

We then climbed into the air at a speed of 170 knots.

CHAPTER 16

Flying due west, I set the trim for a climb of 450 feet per minute and, after passing 200 feet AGL (above ground level), told Joey, "Gear up."

At this, he flicked the landing gear switch into the up position. There was a slight clang as the wheels entered their enclosures, and it gave the plane an extra five knots airspeed. Then, at 1,000 feet AGL, I decided to turn the plane on a northernly direction. My reasoning was we knew that many US cities had likely suffered the same fate as Toronto. So if we headed south, we would likely just run into more zombies. The same would be the likely scenario if we headed west or east, given that we were below the 49th parallel.

It was near dusk when we had to retreat, so I would be flying at night. This wasn't normally a problem, but since airports and cities all seemed to be without power, it was going to be hard to navigate. Joey and I had found some of the pilots' charts (maps) and used them to try and look up places to land. I had to rule out Huntsville Airport where I had started my journey, as I knew there was no one in the town. I couldn't use the property around my cabins, as the grass would likely be soft from melting snow and the lake of course required a plane that was on floats. So I targeted Sudbury, Ontario; programmed the coordinates for the airport into autopilot; and set our altitude for 18,000 feet ASL (above sea level).

Rashad came forward into the flight cabin and reported that Joshua's wife was terribly upset that her husband had been left behind, and this was upsetting her small children. Once again, I was going to have to talk to a widow and explain to her why this had happened. Frankly, I had no idea myself. And the phrase, "It was God's will," was really of little to no comfort. I told Joey to monitor the radio and the instruments and gave Rashad my seat as I went back to try and comfort her and explain why her husband had chosen to stay behind. I pointed out the windows, and Rashad understood to keep watch. We were now past Toronto's Pearson Airport, so I didn't think there would be much of a problem, but still.

Going into the cabin, I could hear the crying. Joshua's little daughter broke away from her mom and stood in front of me with her arms raised, wanting me to pick her up. I did, and she immediately sunk her little head into my neck. His son just stood in front of his mom, tears rolling down his cheeks and looked up to me. I put out my right arm to draw him in for a hug and stroked his hair and then slowly made my way to their mom. "Jessica," I said, facing Joshua's widow, "there is nothing I can really say to make this better. Joshua, like John had been wounded by the zombies and would not have lived much longer. His wound was already festering."

"But we could have gotten him to the doctor," Jessica said. "We didn't need to leave him behind like that."

"No. We had no other choice, and he knew it, which was why he insisted I rescue you and the little ones. He was already dead before we had gotten back to the tower. The only way he could ensure your safety and that of the children was to stay behind and fight off the zombies as long as possible so the rest of us could escape." My eyes teared up as I added, "He made the ultimate sacrifice for his family. And though it may not be easy now, that memory should make it easier when you tell his children sometime down the road when they are older and able to understand what he did and why he did it—for the love of his family."

Jessica put her head down into her hands and just kept crying. as tried to comfort her through the hell she had gone through just the day before. Saleem took the two toddlers from me and comforted them, along with her little sister, all of whom had no understanding that their daddies would never again return.

I returned to the cockpit and took over from Rashad, and we three remaining men looked out the windshield as the dusk turned the sky dark. We were now past Huntsville and proceeding north at our chosen flight level of 18,000 feet, the autopilot having leveled off. Then the question came, "What if there is no one at Sudbury?"

I didn't have an answer but figured we would just continue north. I sent out a PAN-PAN message over the emergency frequency on the plane's radio but, for the first hour and a half, got no replies. We had radar on board, but that only gave us information on things like clouds or other objects in the air with us. It didn't tell us where we were. At 18,000 feet, everything would look exceedingly small, and there were no road signs at that height. One lake would often look like any other lake, especially in the dark. So we had truly little to go on to tell us where we were.

There were, however, some navigation radios that we were able to tune into. With this, I was able to triangulate our position approximately. I had cut back on our airspeed and fuel mixture to maximize our flight time capability, but we were still going at over 170 knots. Joey asked why we didn't just fly closer to the ground so we could see some landmarks. I had to explain that the closer we got to the ground, the thicker the air would be, reducing our fuel range. It would also restrict some of our radio transmissions, as well as the navigation radio reception.

We had fallen below half tanks of fuel when I guessed we were around Sudbury, and only had maybe three hours of fuel left when we finally got a reply to our PAN-PAN call. It was the control tower up in

Timmins, Ontario, and we all broke out in applause and cheers. It was the first contact with the outside world we'd had in a couple of weeks.

I radioed our situation and approximate location and requested a DF (direction finder) steer to their active runway. A DF steer meant the tower would locate you from your radio transmission and then give you the bearing necessary to reach the airport. With this information, I figured we were about an hour south of Timmins and was informed there were no airports south of them open. The zombies had gotten as far north as North Bay and maybe farther; reports were sketchy. We were cleared to land at Timmins but had to remain on the plane, they told us.

Questioning this, we were informed we would be quarantined for seven days to ensure we weren't carrying any of the virus that was causing the mutations to zombies. I stressed the fact we had young children on board and asked how the virus was spread so we could ascertain if any of us maybe had it. The only thing the controller was able to say was, if we had any infections, we would quickly know but otherwise was unable to answer that question. I informed the controller we were all in good health and uninjured from our battles with the zombies. He gave us permission to land but again stated we would be quarantined for the first week on the plane. I requested that, somehow, we be given some food and water supplies, especially for the children. We had gotten supplies while on the expedition in Toronto but only loaded a box or two on the plane before we had to retreat, not nearly enough for five adults, one child, three toddlers, and a dog. We would also need milk for the children. The controller hemmed and hawed for several minutes while confirming our DF steer and then said they would leave some supplies in a hangar that we would be secluded to. He also informed us the city was under martial law, so if we tried to leave the hangar before getting the all clear, we would be shot. It wasn't what one would expect as a welcome, but then these weren't normal circumstances either.

Half an hour later, I was getting everyone strapped in for landing. Joey, not relenting his right seat as my copilot, he watched as I lowered the flaps. Then as I lined up with the runway, I told him, "Gear down." He immediately flicked the landing gear switch to the down position and kept a lookout on our right side for any other aircraft. We were the only plane in the air, but it gave him something of value to do.

As I crossed the threshold of the runway, I cut our power and glided the thirty feet down to a smooth landing. We were met at the end of the runway with a firetruck and a military Humvee, which then guided us to a hangar. Once inside, I shut down our engines, and the armed guards closed the hangar doors, putting us mostly in the dark.

Though the Cessna 401 was an executive plane with fine leather reclining seats, it wasn't spacious enough for nine people and one dog, but we made do.

On the third day of our confinement, over the radio we were introduced to the military commander for the region, General Mac Neil. I nearly had a heart attack when he introduced himself. He went straight to what he considered the point. He wanted to know how we'd escaped Toronto and how many zombies we had killed along the way. I recounted for him my contacts first in the mall and then the Sail store and my rescue of the two families.

After two days of questioning, we got down to the final battle before we'd made good our escape. The general was extremely interested in my approximation of the number of zombies in the city and if I thought there were still more civilians left in the city. He sounded somewhat aghast when I retold him of my rescue of those two families that I hadn't checked the entire building to see if there were other survivors. I didn't find this surprising, as I had known the general from long ago—when he was just out of military college and a young 2nd lieutenant. I shall just say, we hadn't met eye to eye then, so I didn't expect we would now.

Over the remaining few days we were in quarantine, Mac Neil continued to debrief me about the situation in Toronto. Then finding out who I was and recalling our past, he informed me he'd been presented with 7,500 troops with orders to take back Toronto and the surrounding area from the zombies. At this time, we estimated the zombie strength to be at somewhere between 100,000 to 250,000. At best he'd be outnumbered thirteen to one; it sounded like a suicide mission to me. I shared as much detail as I could.

We Toronto survivors finally got a clean bill of health. So finally, stinking to high heaven, we deboarded our plane. We all got some hot showers and fresh food and donated clean clothes.

When we were refreshed, I was summoned to see the general face-to-face. In his war room, he told me he was sorry for any wrong he'd done me those many years ago but that he had been a young fresh officer and inexperienced. Then he showed me the map of his plan to retake Toronto. He would need to travel over seven hundred kilometers, and much of that could be behind zombie lines. He couldn't risk bypassing any groups of zombies on his way, for the zombies could then encircle his troops. But did they have the mind to do something like that? He needed to know. Going over my accounts of contacts yet again, we concluded they did somehow have organization in their purpose, so an ambush was likely.

The discussion then went to how the Americans were dealing with the crisis. The general told me they had bombed several of their own cities, as they were overrun by zombies. There was no way to know how many zombies were killed or, worse, how many civilians they'd killed themselves. We were going to try and avoid that mistake. But with only 7,500 men, it was going to be a very uphill battle.

I suggested that, if we could bring in part of the force from the south, we would be able to catch them in a pincher move with most of the force coming in from the north.

"Where would we be able to hold a staging area?" the general inquired.

"We/you could land a force of men on the Toronto Islands, as the last we knew, they were only lightly inhabited by zombies. Take in a small strike team to secure the islands. Then it can be joined by a larger force of, say, 1,000 men. We can then use the airport tunnel and ferries to launch a daylight attack on the city and do house-to-house clearing of zombies. We must hit early in the morning, just after sunrise with the main force. But the strike team can be in a day earlier. The remainder of the force will then attack from the north over an eighty- to one hundred-kilometer front. You will be spread thin, but it should provide a wide enough corridor that the two forces will be able to meet up relatively safely. From there, you can then spread out east and west to clean up any small groups of zombies."

"What will you need for the strike force?" the general asked.

"Whoa, I never said I was going back to Toronto, General."

"It is your plan, and I do think it will work."

"But I'm not in the army anymore, General. And besides, I have a commitment to the two men's families that I have out of there—their safety and well-being."

"How safe or well are they if the zombies aren't stopped? We have a plan, and we are obligated to try to save our country. Once a soldier, always a soldier. It's in your blood; it's what you're meant to do."

I considered this and then quietly exited the room. I walked over to the hotel that was putting us up and up to my room and to George. Talking to George, I relayed what had been discussed with the general, not noticing the door to my balcony was open.

"Could I come with you?" Joey asked.

I was startled to see him there standing in the doorway and just looked at him while petting George's head. "No," I said. "You need to stay and help take care of your mother and sisters."

"But Rashad and Saleem can do that. I want to stay with you, I'm your copilot, remember?"

How could I forget? He had been the second-best copilot I'd ever had. I got up off the bed and walked over to him. We both went out on the balcony, my arm around his young shoulder. "It's a mission that needs to be done," I told him. "I'm a hunting guide. And yes, I know the prey and the area, so I am the natural choice."

Joey swung around in front of me and gave me a huge hug. Then looking up at me, he said, "Just promise you will come back."

I hugged him back. Then looking over the nearby lake, I told him, "You and your family and Joshua's family is why I have to do this. I have lived a full life and had children. But I no longer know if they are alive or dead. I need to try and make this world safe for you and the other children. I can only promise I will try and come back."

George had now joined us and was sitting alongside us.

CHAPTER 17

The next morning, I joined the general and several of his senior staff for a briefing. It was there when I found out what resources we were going to have. In addition to the 7,500 troops, he had eight CH-147 Chinook helicopters and six CH-146 Griffon helicopters. He also had five CC-130 Hercules aircraft and four Apache gunships. He proposed the starting point of Sudbury, which wasn't too bad. But I pointed out that the southern strike force was going to need air cover, as well as using the Chinooks for transportation. This would be putting the Chinooks at their maximum range to Toronto Island and back to Sudbury, as well as way over the range of the Griffons, which I figured for our air support. The general than asked what I would suggest.

We weren't sure how far north the zombies had penetrated, having only seen the two on that video that had started my journey. I suggested using the Apache gunships to fly out a flanking movement and use Huntsville as our base of operations. The main force could follow the highways down from Sudbury and North Bay, supported by the Apache and Griffons. This would then put the Griffons within range of Toronto to provide air support. It would take likely a day to secure the area north of Huntsville, and my hunt camp would be able to serve as a HQ (headquarters).

The general gave this some thought and then conferred with his staff officers. He then introduced Major Frank Harding, who would be leading an Airborne regiment assault of 350 men. This was to be the first section of our strike force. In discussions with the major, he stated he and his men would need a safe location to land. I suggested that I could lead in a small team to secure the Toronto Islands as well as the airport. We could then secure a safe area for the Airborne's landings. We decided on using the exhibition grounds, as they would give lots of room.

I was assigned a team of forty men, and the general gave me a field commission as a captain. So, I said to the collective staff to recap, "My team is to land on the Toronto Islands and secure the airport there, as well as all the islands and the island ferries. Then we'll secure the docking point on the mainland for the ferries, as well as the tunnel to the airport. We'll next secure the exhibition grounds for the landings of the Airborne, all within twenty-four hours, shortly followed by the rest of the strike force via Chinooks."

"Actually, Captain, you will have only six hours to secure the exhibition grounds and ten hours to secure all the islands," General Mac Neal said, "as well as the ferry docks."

I dropped the pointer I had been using and just stared at him for several seconds, but it seemed an eternity. "You haven't learned much over the years have you, General?"

"The speed of our actions is imperative. We have to secure Toronto and Southern Ontario if we are to win this war. We need to eradicate the zombies before they can eradicate us."

"We will be outnumbered something like fifteen to one, sir. And this enemy has no qualms about dying, as they are already dead. I want to talk to my command. I will only except volunteers, since this will likely be our first and last mission, sir."

That afternoon for the first time, I met the young men who were now under my command. I began the meeting by reading the poem "Charge of the Light Brigade":

95

Half a league, half a league
Half a league, Onward
All in the Valley of Death
Rode the six hundred

"Well, gentlemen, it appears we are to be the light brigade. Though we won't be six hundred, our fate is still likely the same. Many of you—or rather, many of us—will not be coming back. Our task is to secure several positions, and we have only ten hours to do it. We will be broken into four sections—A, B, C, and D sections. A and B will be on copter number one, while C and D will be on copter number two.

"Copter one will land on the Toronto Island at the airport. Their task will be to secure said airport from any zombies. Once the airport is secured, section A will stay behind to defend the airport and the tunnel entrance. Section B will then proceed to the exhibition grounds to secure it for the Airborne, which will be coming in on our heels some six hours later.

"Copter two will land at Ward's Island, and C and D sections will clear and secure Ward's Island and Center Island, after which they will secure the ferry for the rest of the strike team. You men in copter two will have to do some house-to-house clearing. And then section C will need to go over to the ferry docks on the mainland and hold that position. What do we have in terms of armaments?" I directed my question to my 2IC (second in command).

"Each man will be equipped with standard rifles with 200 rounds of ammunition, as well as scope sighting and the ability for both automatic fire and semiautomatic fire. Plus, we will have six M60 machine guns, each with five boxes of belt-fed ammunition."

"Good. But increase the M60 ammunition to ten boxes and five hundred rounds. Do we have any flamethrowers?"

"Well, that's kind of World War II stuff."

"Yeah, but also heavily used in the Vietnam War, as well as Korea. And fire destroys more zombies than bullets do. Men, while I'm at it, also remember you need to take headshots. Body shots will do nothing for the most part. Get us some flamethrowers."

"How many do you think we'll need?"

"See if you can lay your hands on ten, plus extra tanks. Anyone have any questions about our missions?"

There was a low murmur, but no one spoke out.

"Fine, then we leave at 0500 hours tomorrow. And may God help us all."

I returned to the hotel and was confronted in the lobby by the two families I had rescued—or what was left of them.

"You're going back?" Saleem asked.

"I have to. I still don't know what happened to my kids. I need to find out their fates."

"Then we go back with you."

"No, you can't go back with me. Don't you understand? That is what your husbands and fathers gave their lives for—so you all could remain safe. Going with me would dishonor their sacrifice. And who would look after the little ones? We all have our destinies in life, and this is where ours part."

I gave each of the children one last hug and continued on to my room.

At 0400 hours the next morning, I was up and getting dressed in combat fatigues. I had three eggs and sausage for breakfast and a hot chocolate. George was staying by my side, and I wasn't sure I wanted to take him on this journey, as it was likely to be my last. Finally, as I began to walk to my strike team, I stopped at the doors for the families and told George he was to stay and watch over the children. At first, he sat and then tried to follow me again, but I ordered him back. As I left the hotel, I ran into the major who then handed me several full magazines for both the Desert Eagle and my Browning. Now as a captain, I raised my hand in salute.

The pilots have already started up the generators to start their choppers as I approached. The ramp was down, ready for loading. The sergeant who I had assigned to get the flamethrowers showed me the armaments already stowed aboard, and then we started loading our troopers. At 0458 hours, we closed the ramp and began on our journey to take back Toronto. In addition of the forty men, we also carried on a sling under our belly fuel tanks with ten thousand gallons of avgas. This was to assist our Chinooks and Griffons with refueling till we got power restored in the city or at least at the airport.

It was past 0830 hours when we finally arrived at Billy Bishop Airport, chopper one landing on the tarmac area and chopper two circling and landing to the east on Ward's Island. We had disembarked within twenty seconds but found no zombies. I went up to the control tower, where I found the M60 machine gun we had commandeered. Beside it lay Joshua with an apparent self-inflicted bullet wound to his head. I sat heavily into one of the controller's chairs, pulled my hands up over my head, and sobbed.

The sergeant reported everything secure on the airport side of the island, so I told him to get two men for a burial detail while the rest of section A continue to the mainland side of the tunnel. The tunnel was now in total darkness again, all lighting extinguished. We lit a few glow sticks, and section A started to build a defensive position around the mainland entrance to the tunnel while section B and I went on to the CNE grounds. So far, we had met no resistance from any zombies, so we were entering the Princess Gates by just after 9:00 a.m. We now had just three and a half hours to secure the site for the Airborne landing.

Things were going well till we tried to enter the colosseum to secure it. That was where we had our first firefight with somewhere between seventy-five to a hundred zombies inside. We immediately engaged the zombies. It seemed, though they were in a large number, they didn't put up much of a fight. The only drawback was when my men tried to shoot them in the bodies; I had to yell at them to shoot for the heads.

We had cleared the building in only twenty-five minutes. We then left four men to watch over the area where the midway went, and the rest of us went on to clear the other buildings. To optimize time, we split up into threes and went through the buildings we found to be open—among them the food building and the home living building—and found several other buildings, locked so we figured the zombies couldn't get inside those buildings any more than we could.

We were now down to an hour before the Airborne arrived and did a radio check on how sections C and D were doing. They had come across maybe fifty zombies hiding in the homes on Ward's Island and another twenty-five in Centerville, the amusement portion of Center Island. Section C then split up, with six men patrolling the islands and the other four going with section D to secure the mainland side of the ferry landing.

As we heard Major Harding's Hercs passing overhead and watched the paratroopers begin their jumps, Corporal Mann was watching the Dufferin Gates and reported zombies were massing just north of the gates. Five of us went to assist the corporal to keep the landing zone secure. We had one flamethrower with us, so we ignited its nozzle and began to spray the chemical fire over the horde approaching. Fire engulfed the first row of zombies; they were coming about ten abreast. The second wave also lit up like Roman candles. We now fired on any that were not stopped by the flamethrower. But because we still had a good distance between them and us, we were able to take the time and aim for good shots. Then we heard that zombies were attacking at the Princess Gates. They appeared to be using an organized attack, and most of the Airborne still hadn't even reached the ground.

We switched to rapid fire and began dropping more and more zombies, but they just kept coming at us. As the paratroopers began to land, they joined in the fight. The firefight lasted half an hour, but we sustained no casualties.

Then over the radio we got a call—zombies were attacking the ferry docks on the mainland. The troops had set up two of the M60 machine guns and were mowing many down, but without the headshots, they weren't killing as many as they shot down. Those shot just seemed to get back up after a few minutes. We, at that time, had no vehicles to reinforce our men at the docks. But just off the CNE grounds on the waterfront was the old Ontario Place. Long deserted, it still had a marina so section B, plus fifty of Major Harding's men, boarded some boats and, with a flotilla, joined the men from section D at the docks to fight off this zombie horde. We had been able to hold our ground before, but another horde was attacking the airport and section A. These attacks seemed very much to have a level of intelligence about them, something we hadn't expected from zombies.

Since it had become clear that, just shooting the zombies without being able to guarantee the headshots, we were making really very little headway, I spoke to the major. I suggested we incinerate those we had put down with the flamethrowers and inform command that this was what we needed to do. That way, the reinforcements could bring along many flame-throwers and replenishing tanks.

Command radioed back that the first wave of reinforcements were already Airborne but further reinforcements would be so armed. We planned to have the first wave land on the islands, three at the airport and the other five on Center and Ward's Islands. It was another two hours before the first wave arrived, and though the attacks by the zombies seemed to be organized, they didn't attack in large numbers. At the time, I told the major that was good, but we could expect much larger numbers after sunset. With now nearly six hundred men on the ground, the second wave having also landed, we were able to spread out a good perimeter, securing a large amount of the lakefront west of Young Street to Jamison.

That night, as expected, the zombies began to attack in force, first with only a couple hundred, which we easily destroyed, but then coming at us from all directions in the thousands. The battle raged all night, with swarm after swarm just coming at us. At first, my unit had been placed on reserve. But since we were the only ones with flamethrowers, we were quickly put back into action as the zombies began breaching some of the defensive positions. No sooner would we be able to plug one breach than they would breach on the other side of our defense, running my men ragged.

By sunrise, the next day we counted nearly a hundred of our men dead or dying, five from my unit, and estimated we had killed nearly ten thousand zombies. The air reeked of burning flesh, and we had no choice but to burn our own dead. It was a major dilemma for our wounded, as we knew of no cure from the virus of the zombies and had to ascertain whether the wounds were a result of entanglement with a zombie or had another cause. If it were another cause, then we thought we could save them. Those wounded from engagement with a zombie we quietly put out of their misery and then burned. It was a hard decision for a doctor or field medic to make, but it had to be done to close down the infections.

On the northern front, the general had dispatched the first wave of four thousand men with support of four Apache and four of the Griffon helicopters, his main forces following down some of the major highways and clearing all the towns. He had set up his HQ in Huntsville at my hunting camp as suggested, and the two families I had rescued had gone with him, telling him correctly that I had promised them safety and homes on my lands. They would help as domestics for the general, doing some cooking and cleaning. When I heard this, I didn't much like the idea of them serving the general. But they had worked as domestics before, and frankly, so had members of my family. So I couldn't think down on them. It also gave them a chance to keep informed about how the battles were going.

With fresh reinforcements and a lull in the fighting, my team finally got some rest after over twenty-four hours of action. We were aroused again at noon, though. My, our, next assignment was to clear the subway system of any zombies, as this would be a means for them to come up behind us in attack. Our main force had now secured the area from the Don River to the east, Queen Street to the north, and Dufferin/Jamison to the West. It was slow going, but the men were clearing building by building above ground. However, where some thought we could still be vulnerable was in the subway system running under the city. It was also thought to be dark in the tunnels so a perfect place for the zombies to hide during the day.

I pointed out to Major John Syndale, another of the general's staff and commander of the Central Toronto Force, that the subway system had at least four routes, not to mention the sidelines for taking a subway out of service, and I was now down to only thirty-five men. He agreed and assigned me fifteen more men and set the goal for my unit to clear all the stations north up to Bloor Street, where we'd also get the east/west subway line. This still meant I would have to divide my forces into two parts, one going up the Yonge line and the other going up the University line.

CHAPTER 18

With the fifteen replacements, I went back to inform my crew of our latest orders—that we were to clear the subway lines as far north as Bloor Street. "We will be in near total darkness due to the lack of power. But, on the other hand, we don't have to worry about being electrocuted by the third rail. We will use glow sticks, flares, and flashlights to light our way. Because we are going to go up both the Yonge line and University/Spadina line, we will be divided into two groups. We'll try to maintain radio contact, but being underground may pose a problem there. Any questions?"

Corporal James raised his hand and, when I acknowledged him, asked, "What armaments will we have, sir?"

"We will be carrying our standard rifles, with 200 rounds of ammunition. Plus each section will carry five flamethrowers. Be sure we have full tanks."

"What about the M60s?"

"The tunnels will actually be too narrow for them to be really effective. We will travel with a point man protected by two flame-throwers and then, at three meters behind the main force, one flamethrower at the rear in case we do miss anything. Any other questions?

"Then mount up. We leave in ten."

Having the ground forces secured up to Queen Street, we had no problem penetrating the subway system at Union Station, where, as planned, we split into two groups, both heading north along the rails. The lighting was horrific. We couldn't see more than ten feet ahead of us, and the flares, when first lit, would often be blinding. We would throw them first underhanded about seven meters ahead of us and then light a glow stick every few meters as we walked along the tunnel.

I was in the group going up the Yonge line. So, the first station we came to was the King Street Station, where we ran into our first group of zombies. There was only ten of them, and we shot three of them before turning the flamethrowers on the attack. In the dark, it did look like one or two had fled farther up the tunnel. Once we were certain there were no more zombies about, we went and checked all the exits and entrances for that station. Then we moved on. Since we suspected some zombies had fled, we used the flamethrowers to light up the first part of the next tunnel. There was a scream as one zombie lit up in flames.

With the flares and glow sticks lighting our way, we proceeded to the next station, which was Queen. Since this was as far as had been secured, we took our time inspecting the entrances and exits. This station also had exits into places like Eaton Mall, where we found another group of soldiers set to clear that location. Now we were entering the unsecured areas, so every fifty paces or so, the flamethrowers would send out a blast of their chemical flame—just in case something was out ahead of us.

The next station was Dundas Street, where we came across some fifty zombies. We were able to engage them on the platforms, and due to the narrowness of those platforms, the flamethrower could just light them up row after row. It only took five minutes to clear that station. However, we did sustain our first injury when one man fell off the platform and broke an arm. He was able to continue with the fight. I was hoping that would be the full extent of our casualties, but later that day, my hopes would be dashed.

Since we were now past the ground forces, we padlocked all the entrances to the station as a precaution to prevent the zombies from using the entrances to get behind our troops. We were also able to contact the team on the University line. We found that, like us, they had hit minimum zombie resistance. It seemed the zombies hadn't really found the advantage of the subway system, which was good.

Next was Wellesley Station. Here again we found little resistance. From above ground, we contacted the Central Toronto Force command and gave our report, suggesting they could use the tunnels, as we thought the zombies would to come up behind some of them. Then we could get them in a pincher movement at least along the subway corridors. I was told the suggestion would be taken under consideration.

Now we were approaching our final objective of the day—Bloor/Yonge Station. It consisted of two levels of track, as well as access to an underground mall, plus business offices and condos aboveground. We first contacted a group of about a dozen zombies some hundred meters from the platform. We hit them first with the flamethrowers and then with rifle fire. Then as we made our advance on the station, more zombies started coming at us down the tracks. We brought up two more flamethrowers to help support us and continued firing into the tunnel.

Our forward advance was stalled due to the sheer number of zombies coming down the tracks. Their volume even forced us to fall back. The heaviness and bulk of the flamethrowers tanks caused one of the lead flamethrowers to be overrun by the zombies; three other riflemen met the same fate.

With light primarily from only the glow sticks, we dug in our positions in the tunnel, hiding behind the pillars and shooting what zombies came close till they stopped coming. Having regrouped, I led my remaining twenty men back up the tracks till we got to the station platform. There, I sent five men with one flamethrower to the north end of the station, using the overhanging ledge as their cover. Once they were there, we attacked the zombies on the platform from both sides, trapping many in the middle. However, we lost another two of those five men to a zombie attack coming in from north of the station.

Having now secured that platform, I ordered two riflemen and a flamethrower to keep watch of the northern tracks while I led the rest up to the next level. There, we again met an estimated hundred zombies. Our first attempt to gain the platform was repulsed, and I tried to contact either the rest of the main force or my other team going up the University line without success.

I was now down to a lucky thirteen men, including myself, and we were starting to run low on ammunition as well as chemicals for the flamethrowers. With two flamethrowers to lead the way, I ordered my men to ready for hand-to-hand combat. And like the Light Brigade, we charged up to the platform firing with full magazines. We shot zombies at point-blank range, blowing away their skulls or faces; smashed their heads in with the butts of our rifles; and set fire to dozens—all to take that platform and secure the station.

The battle for the Bloor/Yonge Station took a total of an hour and a half, with an estimated two hundred zombies destroyed. At the end of it all my section had lost a total of fifteen men going up Younge Street bringing only ten survivors to continue.

An hour after the fight ended, we got a hundred reinforcements, men and women who were to take the streets above and begin the pincher movement I had suggested. The general also sent another one thousand men being held in reserve to assist clearing the city of the zombies. The men I had sent along the University line had also run into heavy resistance once they'd reached the east/west cross line and came out with fourteen men, having lost eleven. Command then assigned us more men to continue clearing the subway, with a renewed force of twenty-five men for each subway line, some going east, some going west, and still two groups going to the north till all the stations were secured.

I again was given a command of what we now called subway rats, and we proceeded east of the Bloor Station with the goal of reaching all the way to Kennedy Station, engaging the zombies many times along the way. We then fought our way through to Castle Frank Station as another evening came upon us. We decided to hold up there, rather than try to converse the viaduct in the dark.

The next morning as the sun rose, we proceeded on to the Broadview Station, where we again engaged zombies while high above the Don River valley. We lost two more men plunging to their deaths in the valley below but battled through and then made our way to the next station and the next.

When we reached Greenwood Station, where there was a subway maintenance yard off to the south, we ran into a few hundred zombies. That battle took about an hour and a half, and we lost six more men.

It took a week to get to Kennedy Station in the subway and ten days for the aboveground forces to take back all of Toronto with yet another five hundred of the reserves. But the northern strike team had cleared their area and joined up with the Toronto team twelve days into the campaign, with a total of thirty-eight thousand people rescued and an estimated one hundred thousand zombies destroyed. The combined strike force of 7,500 men and women had a loss of just over 500 of their numbers.

As I boarded the Griffon helicopter that would return me to my hunt camp, my mind went back to Lord Tennyson's poem that summed so well the sacrifice of these people The Charge of the Light Brigade:

Then they rode back but not but not the six hundred
While horse and hero fell, they that had fought so well,

Came through the jaws of death, back from the mouth
of Hell,
All that was left of them,
Left of the six hundred

I remembered the men who'd come with me into the subway, the young men to whom I'd recited that poem. I'd told them that likely half of them would not return, and unfortunately I had been correct, though like many commanders I'd hoped to be wrong. I was weary and full of regret for the lives lost—so much so I couldn't see the helmeted pilot of my helicopter as I closed my eyes and we rose into the air.

Thirty minutes into the flight, one of the crew handed me a headset so I could speak to and hear from the pilot. My eyes shot wide as we neared my camp and I heard the voice over the intercom.

"I heard you had some excitement back there in the subway," the pilot said with a laugh. It was a voice I had thought I would never hear again—the voice of my son; he had survived and was now flying for the rescue missions.

Tears formed in my eyes and joy in my heart as we landed on the grass runway of my property. There I was met by Joey, along with George and Saleem. They were quickly joined by Rashad and his mother, as well as the other children. Yes, I had lost many young lives like the six hundred, but I had also saved many lives, and this was what it was all about.

It still took the general another three months to completely rid Southern Ontario of all the zombies. But from the 38,000 we'd rescued in Toronto alone; he was able to gain an additional 10,000 volunteers. How they did south of the border is anyone's guess, but we had to now defend the longest undefended border for several years.

ABOUT THE AUTHOR

The author is a survivalist having served in the Canadian Army for a combined 13 years (Reserve and Active Duty). After leaving the service he went on to complete a BA at Trent University in Psychology/Sociology, his pilot license, and a diploma in Teaching Adults. It was learned while at university that he had a severe learning impediment in both reading and writing. To overcome this challenge in his life, he became an avid member of the local libraries as well as taking Creative Writing courses and submitting some of his short works to competitions to earn honorary mentions. This first novel of his is the culmination of those efforts.

Printed in the United States
by Baker & Taylor Publisher Services